MARIGOLDS AND MURDER

PORT DANBY COZY MYSTERY #1

LONDON LOVETT

Happy Reading!

♡ London Lovett

Marigolds and Murder

Copyright © 2017 by London Lovett

ISBN-13: 978-1976216169

ISBN-10: 1976216168

CHAPTER 1

I stepped back to admire my handiwork. I wasn't exactly Van Gogh, but I had to admit, the tiny flowers I'd painted on the rustic bench were charming. I'd found the old bench at a yard sale and had decided that it would look great under the bay window, still leaving enough room for me to roll out my flower carts and set up my portable 'specials and deals' chalkboard.

Aside from falling in love with the eclectic charm of Port Danby, I'd fallen instantly in love with the small building I'd leased for my shop, Pink's Flowers. Like every shop on Harbor Lane, it was entirely unique with its Cape Cod shingles and deep bay window. While not exactly traditional for the Cape Cod style, I'd had the wood siding painted a blush pink because . . . well . . . it *was* Pink's Flowers. The thick window trim and the French door for the entry were painted bright white for a perfectly pleasing contrast. The unusual pink color had drawn a few judgmental glances from neighboring shop owners, but once everything was finished, people seemed to approve.

I dipped my paintbrush into the bottle of lavender paint, and as I pulled it out, my phone rang, startling me and triggering a small string of calamities. Pale purple paint dripped down my shin. I stepped sharply to the side to avoid more and kicked the paint bottle. It fell over and splashed across my sandal and foot. I flirted with the idea of not answering my phone, but I knew it was my mom. If I didn't answer, her head would fill with endless terrifying scenarios that might be keeping her daughter from answering the phone.

Standing with my knee lifted and my purple foot high off the ground, I managed to keep my balance as I picked my phone up off the window ledge. "Hey, Mom, can I call you back? I've got a purple foot."

"What? Why? Did you bruise it? Are you having circulation problems? Maybe your shoes are too tight." My mom was highly skilled at dashing off numerous opinions and unnecessary advice without needing to stop for a breath.

"It's purple paint, Mom. My shoes and circulatory system are fine."

"Well, why didn't you tell me? You gave me a fright." I didn't need to see through the phone to know she was placing her hand against her chest for added drama.

"I would have told you if you hadn't jumped right into your list of possible sources and solutions for a purple foot." I decided to give delaying the call another shot. "Let me call you back."

"I'm just calling to see how things are going with the little flower store." She couldn't have said the words with more disappointment if she'd punctuated each one with a sniffle. But I couldn't fault her for that. My poor mom, the eternal optimist and the woman who took huge pleasure in bragging to her book club about her daughter's successes, had suffered the trifecta of motherly letdowns. In the past few years, I'd quit medical school and walked out on a six figure job in the perfume industry. But the last disappointment was the one that really had the poor woman reeling.

I braced my free hand against the window ledge to keep my balance. "The *little* flower store is fine. I open in two weeks. My right leg is getting tired. Can I call you back?"

"You need better shoes." I opened my mouth to remind her of the painted foot but decided it would be a waste of breath. "Lacey, have you heard from Jacob?"

I made sure to huff in annoyance loud enough that she could hear me. "Why would I hear from him? We aren't together anymore, and mentioning him in every phone call is not going to magically bring him back into my life."

Jacob was the third horse in the trifecta. He was like the Kentucky Derby of disappointing blows for my mom. He was rich and handsome and from a *good* family. Unfortunately, that *good* family forgot to teach him that if you were engaged to one woman, it wasn't *good* to date another woman. Jacob's family owned Georgio's Perfume, a multimillion dollar fragrance company, and for one year I had been employed as their head perfumer. I had been born with hyperosmia, or in more crude terms, a heightened sense of smell. Sometimes I considered it a gift, and sometimes it was a curse. In the matter of my ex-fiancé, it had been both. Jacob had hired me because I could detect the slightest aroma and even separate that microscopic odor into its basic parts, a skill that made me highly sought after in the perfume industry. But the man had somehow forgotten that skill when he started showing up wearing hints of another woman's perfume on his shirts. And whoever she was, she wasn't even wearing Georgio Perfume.

"I just worry that you were too hasty in your decision to break it off. Jacob was such a nice man."

"He was seeing other women behind my back. How does that make him nice? If you like him so much, give him a call. I'm sure as long as you make sure Dad has new batteries in the remote, frozen entrees in the freezer and plenty of bait in his tackle box, he won't even notice you missing." I hopped toward the door of the shop to go inside and clean my foot.

"Lacey Sue Pinkerton," she said in her best angry mom voice.

"Uh oh, the middle name is coming out. I'm in trouble." I opened the door and hopped clumsily inside. Kingston pulled his sharp black beak out from under his wing. He looked angry about having his nap interrupted.

"You sound funny. Are you exercising, Lacey?"

"Yes, Mom, I'm in the middle of an aerobics class."

"That's enough, miss smarty pants." Apparently we'd moved from middle name use to the good ole smarty pants stand by. I was twenty-eight, but a five minute conversation with my mom and I was back in sixth grade.

"I'm sorry, Mom. I would love to stay on the phone and rehash all the crummy stuff that has befallen me lately, but I need to get back to work."

"Lacey, sweetie, I worry you'll get terribly bored in a small town like Port Dancy."

"Port Danby, and I won't be bored. I'll be running a business."

"Yes, a flower shop. It's quite a change from your life in the big city working with important people."

"It's a big change, Mom. And it's the change I wanted. Besides, I'm looking forward to living in a place where the biggest thing to happen is the neighborhood stray cat knocking over a trash can. There's something to be said for peace and tranquility." Her last words had gotten to me a bit. The notion of life moving too slowly in Port Danby had crossed my mind more than once. But I was determined to keep myself and my mind occupied.

The paint had dried on my foot, caking into a lavender patch on my skin. I lowered the foot to the ground. "I'll call you later, Mom. Kiss Dad for me."

"All right. Call if you need anything."

I hung up and glanced around at my shop. I couldn't help but smile. It was the first time in my working life that I'd gotten to make all the decisions, and I was pleased with the outcome. Cape Cod exterior aside, I went totally batty trying to decide whether to go modern industrial or Soho chic inside. As is often the case, I couldn't make up my mind, so I went with both and invented my own Soho Industrial Chic. Practicality played a big part too. I left the exposed brick walls in place for the corner that was home to the steel rolling shelves I'd purchased at a factory sell off. They were the perfect place to store vases, glassware and ceramic pots. A long antique potter's table took up more than half of the back wall. The deep porcelain basin sink left behind by Elsie, the baker, when she moved her kitchen next door was the perfect place for transferring plants and arranging bouquets.

For a change of pace, I covered the brick wall on the other half of the shop with smooth plaster and bright white paint. An array of wood crates were nailed, bottom side, to the wall to create geometric cubbies for some of the prettier baubles I had for sale. The center of the store held my prize find, a massive island with a black and white checked tile counter and rows of drawers to keep ribbons, tissue and all the small goodies needed in a flower shop. I'd painted the entire island in black chalkboard paint so I could write labels on the drawers.

Kingston, my pet crow, fluttered his large wings a few times, vibrating the ribbons hanging from spools on the wall. I grabbed a bag of sunflower seeds from the top drawer of the island and tossed a few into the dish on his perch. He busied himself with the treat as I stroked the silky black feathers on his head.

"Well, Kingston, the shop is almost ready. I think we're going to like it here. What do you think?"

Kingston flicked the empty shells out of the dish.

"Right, I guess you'll be happy as long as there are plenty of treats."

CHAPTER 2

*P*utting to good use the free trial month yoga class I'd attended, I somehow managed to get my foot into the sink and free of its purple tattoo. Getting it back out took a little more effort. I wrangled my leg away from the basin and patted it dry with a rag.

A gasp shot from my mouth as I spun around and found Elsie standing just a few feet away.

"My gosh, Elsie, you scared me. You move like a cat wearing slippers."

"I've told you many times, you need a bell on the door." Elsie could rival my mom when it came to giving advice and opinions. She pointed her finger, which meant more advice was on its way. "Lola mentioned that her parents sent her a box of old goat bells for the antique shop. That would be perfect."

"You're right. I'll go across the street later and buy one."

Elsie spent her entire day baking and creating the kind of confections that went straight to the thighs, but she was as fit and trim as an Olympian. Even though Elsie was, as she liked to say, 'pushing sixty' (*although Lola had told me Elsie'd already pushed sixty several pushes ago*) every afternoon, she pulled on her shorts and athletic shoes and ran the five mile loop from Harbor Lane down to Pickford Way along the beach, and up Culpepper Road. Elsie and her husband, Hank, a traveling salesman who I had yet to meet because he was always *traveling*, had lived in Port Danby for thirty years. Elsie's Sugar and Spice Bakery was a local and tourist favorite. I'd grown so fond of her goodies, I worried that I, too, would have to start running the grueling five mile loop just to stay ahead of my treat consumption.

Elsie stopped at Kingston's perch to admire him, and my crow liked to be admired. "Hello, handsome."

Kingston responded by bobbing his head up and down in approval like a parrot. "He's going to have a head the size of a balloon if you keep calling him handsome. When I put him near a mirror, he'll stand there for hours just flirting with himself." I took a deep whiff. "How is the pumpkin bread turning out?"

Elsie swung around quickly, nearly dislodging the hasty bun of gray peppered hair at the nape of her neck. I hadn't noticed the streak of flour on her cheek until the sun through the window highlighted it. "How did you know I was making pumpkin bread?" She waved away the question and provided her own answer. "That's right. I forgot about you and that incredible sense of smell."

"I've been smelling a lot of cloves, nutmeg, cinnamon and yeast so I figured pumpkin bread. And to be perfectly honest, I saw Tom, from the corner market, deliver a crate of canned pumpkin."

Elsie put her finger against her lips. "Shh. I like to let people think I'm using fresh. I even leave a few pumpkin halves on the work table. I hope that doesn't make me seem terrible."

"Since your baked goods are like an elixir for happiness, I think we can let this one indiscretion go. Besides, who would fault you for using canned pumpkin? You work so hard."

"Thank you, Pink. You're a gem." The people who I'd already grown close to, like Elsie and Lola, had taken to calling me by my nickname, Pink.

"I'll bring you a sample when I have them perfected."

"Looking forward to it."

Elsie ran her fingers along the black and white tiles on the island.

I'd only known her a few weeks, but it was easy to read that she had something on her mind. But before she could part her lips to speak, the door opened and a salty coastal breeze ushered in behind my neighbor on the other side, Lester. Aside from being Elsie's twin brother, Lester was a retired fireman, who had, after a year of golfing, watching television reruns and as he liked to say watching his hair turn white, decided to open up a coffee shop. He was always a fun sight to see in his snowy white hair, brightly colored Hawaiian shirt and sandals. As far as neighbors went, Lester was much quieter and less opinionated than Elsie. His wife died of cancer just ten years into their marriage and he, as Lester himself put it, never found true love again. (*Yes, those men exist, but they are as rare and hard to find as the perfect fitting bra.*)

Lester popped right up with a question for Elsie. "Well, did you ask her?"

"I was just about to until you came bursting in as if the devil were chasing you."

Lester took immediate offense. "I did no such thing. Should I ask her?"

"No, I'll get to it. Stop being pushy." Elsie shook her head my direction. "He was even pushy in the womb."

"What I should have done was push you right out of it," Lester quipped.

I leaned against the center island and crossed my ankles waiting for them to stop arguing about who should do the asking. I had no idea what the burning question was, but I'd found, with Lester and Elsie, it was easier to let them finish their round of sibling rivalry first. Eventually, they'd get to the point. It was usually entertaining to watch, and it made me, all at once, thankful and disappointed that I'd never had a sibling. Of course Elsie always came out the victor because Lester usually just got tired and gave up.

"We were wondering if we could put my three tables out in front of your shop," Elsie blurted so quickly I hadn't realized her statement was directed at me until I noticed they were both looking expectantly at me.

I pushed off the counter. "Oh, you're talking to me. But why would you need to put the tables in front of my shop? Lester already has three tables, and you have plenty of room in front of the bakery."

Lester rolled his eyes at his sister's clumsy approach to the topic. Lester shuffled forward on his sandals. "Here's the thing, Lacey. Since the bakery used to be here in the flower shop—" He cast his blue-gray eyes around. "Nice work in here, by the way."

"Thank you."

"Anyhow, the customers enjoy getting baked goods and then picking up a coffee inside the Hutch to go with their pastry. As it stands now, if they want to finish their breakfast and if my tables are full, they have to walk past your shop to Elsie's tables."

Elsie put her little fists on her slim hips. "Actually, my tables are almost always full first. You get the spillover customers." Elsie leaned her head toward me. "My tables have a nicer paint finish."

"Your chairs wobble," Lester noted.

"There's nothing wrong with my chairs," Elsie insisted. "It's your big head that wobbles. Just look at him. He's always had an oversized head. He's like one of those bobble headed Hawaiian dolls only instead of a grass skirt, he's wearing a flowery shirt. But back to the tables." She returned her attention to me. "You have plenty of space in front of your shop, and Lester and I will make sure the customers pick up after themselves."

"But there won't be much free space." I walked to the back corner where my rolling carts were waiting to be filled with potted flowers. "Once I open up for business, I plan to use these carts to lure people into the shop. I'll be rolling them out onto the sidewalk on nice days. As you can see, they are quite cumbersome. There just won't be room for any tables. Otherwise, I'd be happy to help." I was new to Harbor Lane, the main street for shops and businesses, and I knew I needed to tread lightly and keep up good relationships with the other shop owners. But I couldn't change my business plan just to accommodate my neighbors.

I could see the disappointment in their faces. It seemed Lester was the first to agree that it just wouldn't work. He nodded. "Of course, you need the front of the store for your own wares, Lacey. It was silly and greedy of us to ask." He looked questioningly at Elsie, who reluctantly nodded in agreement.

"Yes, my brother is right. We'll make do with the table space we have. The customers will get used to it. They'll just have to choose which side to sit on."

"Thanks for understanding," I said as I walked toward the door, hoping they'd get the idea and head out. I had much more to do before my opening.

Elsie's face softened and she smiled. "Of course, Pink. And let us know if there's anything we can do to help."

"Thanks." I opened the door for them and watched them walk out. Lester shuffled on his loose fitting sandals back to the Coffee Hutch, and Elsie walked in her usual confident, surefooted manner back to the Sugar and Spice Bakery. Little did I know that the last few moments had been the start of the Great Port Danby Table War. And my *little flower shop* was situated right between the battle lines.

CHAPTER 3

I finished hanging a few pictures on the back wall and decided to head across the street to see if Lola was interested in getting some lunch. With my shop sandwiched between a bakery and a coffee shop and my extra sensitive olfactory neurons, I seemed to be in a constant state of hunger. I'd hoped for a sample of Elsie's pumpkin bread to get me through the morning, but I hadn't seen or heard from either neighbor since I'd put a crimp in their outdoor seating plan.

"King, did you want to go out for a bit?" My crow hadn't left his perch all morning. I was sure he'd be extra antsy tonight if he didn't get some wing time. Harbor Lane, the two lane street that ran along the front of the shops and led eventually to the beach, was lined with deep purple flowering plum trees, providing rich color, shade and a place for Kingston to perch when he wanted to behave like a real crow. Of course, his unexpected visit always sent the local sparrows and smaller songbirds into a frenzy, but Kingston paid them no attention.

The crow ruffled and shook his feathers and eyed the open door. I leaned back waiting for him to swoop past. Instead, he turned away from the door and huddled down for another nap.

I stepped outside and instantly regretted forgetting my sunglasses at home. The early morning coastal fog had long since been replaced by a crisp breeze that carried with it just enough hint of autumn to make me immediately think about pulling my plush throw blankets out of storage. Even with the lovely summer weather long gone, the sun was sparkling out over the water. The view sure beat tall buildings and streets filled with car fumes.

I headed across to Lola's Antiques. Lola was just a year younger than me and she ran the antique store for her world traveling parents. She was funny and clever and sometimes, when she was excited or nervous, she talked fast, so fast her words didn't always come out in the right sequence. I enjoyed her company, and she seemed to enjoy mine. We had become fast friends.

Lola was wearing one of her many rock and roll t-shirts, a Janis Joplin relic, coupled with faded jeans and a black felt fedora. Her curly red hair popped out on all sides from beneath the tight hat. She was busy adjusting two massive fairy tale style pumpkins on a bale of straw, a rustic touch that looked oddly out of place in front of her quaint shop. Lola told me that once her parents had given her the go ahead to update the store, she'd hired a painter to cover what she had termed as the 'gray pallor of death' on the shop's exterior with a pale, smoky blue. The color looked chic and especially lovely with the wide top to bottom windows. The traditional paneled front door, the wide trim running above the windows and the sheer white curtains made the shop look as if it had been plucked up from some Paris street corner and delivered neatly to Port Danby.

Lola leaned back to admire her holiday display. "What do you think? Too hee haw?"

"Not at all. I think it's perfect."

"Good thing you like it." Her brown eyes were the color of cocoa in the midday sun as she turned to look at me. "Since you're right across the street, you'll be looking at it for the rest of October."

"I had not thought about that. But my opinion stays firm. It's festive and it reminds me that I'm going to need to add some little baubles or something to my shop. I've been so busy getting the shop ready for business, I forgot that it would be opening just before Halloween. Maybe some orange and black garland or something across the window. By the way, Elsie mentioned you had some goat bells. I need something for my door."

"Thank goodness. That'll be one bell down. Sometimes I think my parents are losing their minds from spending so much time at thirty thousand feet." Lola reached for the door. "They sent an entire box of rusty old bells. Even the goats were probably happy to see them go."

Lola's dog, a Boxer, lifted his heavy head from the pillow long enough for me to pet him. He was small for a Boxer, the runt of the litter, apparently. His diminutive size had earned him the name Late Bloomer. Fortunately, for the dog, most people just called him Bloomer.

Lola dipped into the back room to retrieve the box of bells. I wandered around the shop. I'd been in it more than a dozen times, but I was sure I still hadn't seen all the hidden treasures tucked in every nook and corner.

As badly as Lola had wanted to update the antique shop, the interior had, for the most part, remained dark and dated, a sharp contrast to the chic exterior. But moving century old glass cabinets, curios and book shelves would have taken more time and money than Lola had for a remodel. Every inch of the shop was brimming with relics and treasures of the past. Floor space was limited to just enough passage for two people to walk side by side, which was probably for the best. According to Lola, the forest green carpeting that covered the entire floor was better left hidden beneath the antiques.

The clang of several bells was followed by the click clack of Lola's boots. She held up a bell with impressive patina and a colorfully fringed leather strap. "This one has the best sound." She rang it again and yelled out in a long, southern drawl. "Come to supper, y'all!"

"Hey speaking of supper, I'm starved. Are you interested in lunch?"

"Yes. Let's go to Franki's Diner. She made some of her corn bread yesterday. It goes great with her chili."

"Sounds yummy." I leaned against the front glass counter and absently fingered the pile of flyers sitting on top of it. "Elsie's been baking pumpkin bread all morning, and my mouth hasn't stopped watering. I thought she'd bring me a taste sample, but I think I upset her."

"Why is Elsie upset? Not that I really care because she's always upset about something. I thought runners were always supposed to be high on those endolphins. She must not be catching many on her run."

"It's endorphins and you don't actually catch them."

Lola walked behind the counter to grab her purse. "Either way, Elsie needs some. What's she upset about?"

"It's nothing really. She and Lester wanted to use some of the space in front of my shop for their tables." I quickly changed subjects not really wanting to talk about Lester and Elsie behind their backs. They had been truly supportive neighbors, and I knew Lola could gnaw away at something if I let her. I picked up a flyer from the stack. "The Port Danby Pumpkin Contest. Biggest pumpkin wins a hundred dollars."

"Yep, welcome to Hokey Town, U.S.A."

"Then call me hokey because I love that I am now living in a town that has a pumpkin growing contest. Do a lot of people enter?"

Lola straightened up her sales receipts. "No, mostly it's just a contest between Beverly Kent and Virginia Hopkins, two elderly widows who live out on Culpepper Road. They're longtime neighbors, but things get pretty un-neighborly between them during pumpkin growing season." She pulled out a receipt. "Speaking of Beverly. I hate to gossip—" she began.

I raised a brow at her to silently question that statement.

"O.K., right. I love to gossip. This morning Willy Jones, the fisherman—" She looked at me for affirmation, but I shrugged my shoulders. "Anyhow, he's an old guy who has a fishing boat down in the marina. He's married to Theresa Jones. They've been married for about a hundred years."

I blinked at her. "Did I mention the starving thing?"

"Right." She put the receipt back on the pile and grabbed her 'closed for lunch' sign. She continued with her story as she hung it. "Well, about a week ago, Theresa brought in a box of old things, and there was a class ring from nineteen tickety two or some other long ago era. It was a nice one with a big blue stone, and it was strung from a thin, feminine chain."

We walked out onto the sidewalk, and I silently hoped her story was going to get more interesting.

"Not sure what school because Port Danby High has a green stone in their senior class ring. Not that I bought one. I mean who wants to wear a big old ring like that on their finger?"

We walked along Harbor Lane. As long as we were heading closer to food, I decided there was no harm in hearing the rest of her story, meaningless details and all.

"Anyhow, Theresa brought in the box of goods, but I didn't have time to go through it all. There were a few old porcelain vases and a framed sampler she said she'd found at an estate sale but nothing too exciting. So I gave her a hundred bucks for the lot, and she left saying she was going to get a manicure and some new face cream with the money."

We walked past the Port Danby Police Station, although it was more just a tiny building with two front windows and two reserved parking spots out front. The Port Danby black and white patrol car rarely left its reserved spot. The second car was a blue sedan with one of those specially marked license plates that an undercover police officer might drive, only they weren't so undercover due to the specially marked plates.

"Let's cross here." Lola interrupted her story long enough to glance back and forth for traffic.

I followed behind her. "Probably not the best idea to jaywalk right in front of the police station."

Lola blew air through her lips. "They don't care unless it's tourist season." We crossed the street and reached the sidewalk in front of the diner.

The outside of Franki's Diner reminded me of an old fashioned train station with a big clock stuck in the center of a stumpy tower that jutted up from a charcoal gray metal roof. White multi-paned doors finished off a long line of symmetrical yellow trimmed windows. Yellow and purple pansies had been haphazardly planted along a thin flower box running the length of the building. They were an odd contrast to the exterior colors. I would have suggested something taller and more pastel like snapdragons. Although snapdragons might not have survived the coastal fog.

"So?" I said managing to make the one syllable sound like a question.

"So?" Lola countered.

I rolled out a heavy sigh. "The ring story? I'm hoping there's more because otherwise there was a lot of build up for nothing."

"Oh yes, the ring. Well, this morning, old Willy came into the shop, huffing and puffing as if he'd run all the way from the marina. He was seriously about to fall over from a stroke. He wanted to know if I'd sold the ring yet." Lola laughed. "As if some century old class ring would be a hot item."

"You do run an antique shop."

"True enough. So I sold him back his own ring and gold chain for twenty bucks and off he went a happy little fisherman. Of course, he made me promise not to tell Theresa. I figure he'll probably give it to Beverly because she was his high school sweetheart back in the day."

Lola reached for the door of the diner.

"Beverly?" I asked.

Lola stopped in the open doorway and looked back at me with an annoyed brow. "The woman on Culpepper Road who grows big pumpkins. Keep up, Pink. That's how this story started. Remember?"

"Actually, I don't remember because it was so long ago."

"Funny woman."

I followed Lola to a table. "Seriously, I think I grew some gray hair in the meantime."

Lola stopped at a table that was halfway down the line of windows. "Will this do, granny gray hair?"

"Yep."

CHAPTER 4

ranki breezed by and dropped two menus on the table. Harried or not, her perfectly sculpted beehive, a hairdo she wore to give the place a fifties flair, had not lost one inch of symmetry. It sat in perfect mid-century glory right on top of her head. "I'll be back in a minute. I'm swamped. Janie called in sick this morning, so I'm basically a one woman show out on the dining floor today." With that rushed narrative, she hurried off to the pick-up window.

I'd only been inside the diner three times, and during those visits I'd learned that Franki Rumple, the proud owner of Franki's Diner, was a single parent, raising four teenagers, two sets of twins. Taylor and Tyler were two lanky sixteen-year-old boys. They were impossible to tell apart, and their names were equally confusing. Franki liked to complain that the only thing they were good at was making trouble, but she always talked about them with a mom's loving twinkle in her eyes. Kimi and Kylie had just turned fourteen, and they seemed to be a little less trouble than the boys. They were also easier to tell apart because Kimi liked to wear purple and Kylie preferred pink. Franki claims that once the second set of twins was born her husband took it as a sign the marriage was cursed and left. I would have taken it as a sign that the man was just a coward, but we all saw people through different lenses.

Lola pored over the slightly greasy menu as if she was making some grand life decision.

"I thought you were going to order the chili." I leafed through the menu too.

"I am. Just thought I'd check in case something better popped out at me." Lola slapped the menu shut, resulting in an air current that made the red curls around her face vibrate. Her nose crinkled as she lifted her hands to her face. "Ugh, I smell like goat. I'm going to just run in and wash up. Order the chili and corn bread for me. And an iced tea with lemon."

"Right. Got it." I decided to have the same.

I sat back and glanced around. The inside of Franki's Diner was a predictable parade of shiny red vinyl, polished chrome and white laminate, but every time I walked in I felt this wonderful sense of nostalgia. At first, I couldn't quite pinpoint the source of it. Then it occurred to me that the red diamond pattern tiles running along the white tile base of the counter were exactly like the pattern in the kitchen of my childhood home. The chain of red diamond tiles brought me back to chilly winter mornings when my mom would lace hot tea with gobs of honey and we would sit and gab and gossip about everything from friends to Aunt Ruth's frightening new hair color. It was funny how small details could so easily take you back in time.

There were a few familiar faces sitting at the other tables. So far I'd only learned the names of the shop owners in close proximity. A woman I'd never seen before was sitting two tables over sawing angrily away at a steak as if the slab of meat had somehow wronged her. She was an elderly woman with chestnut hair and a long thick line of gray roots. Her fingers were red and raw as if she spent a lot of time washing dishes or gardening. The sunburn on her nose seemed to indicate the latter. Whoever she was, she was not having a good day, and neither was the steak on her plate.

Lola returned and slid into the seat just as Franki came over to take our order. She gave her beehive bun a push to center it on her head and looked down at her notepad.

I smiled up at her. "Two orders of chili and corn bread, and two iced teas with lemon."

"That's easy enough." Franki scribbled something on her pad. "And the corn bread is excellent today. I added in some green chili for a little pop of flavor." Franki was one of those people who took pride in her work, and it showed in the quality of her food. I'd also discovered that if you were a new customer, which I was just several visits ago, she liked to hover over the table to see if you approved or not. The first time I came in, I'd ordered a cheese omelet. Franki stood over me, waiting for me to take my first bite. As I carried the eggs to my mouth, I worried that I wouldn't like it and then I'd have to force a cheery smile, spout false accolades and continue eating it. Fortunately, it was delicious.

"I'll be right back with your chili." Franki scurried off on her sensible nurse style shoes.

The rather angry woman several tables over was still terrifying her food with a steak knife. I tapped Lola's foot and glimpsed past her shoulder. "Don't turn around but who is the growly, grumbly woman sitting two tables over? She looks upset."

Naturally, as was always the case when someone was told not to turn around, Lola twisted back to look at the woman. She turned back around looking disappointed as if she'd expected something far more exciting than a woman sawing at her food. "Oh her." Lola sat forward to speak softer. "That's Virginia Hopkins."

I waited for more, but Lola's focus was drawn away to the sugar packets. "I think I'll try this Steve stuff to see if it's the same as sugar."

"I think it's called Stevia, and it's not the same as sugar. Only sugar tastes like sugar. So why is Virginia Hopkins so angry?"

Lola shoved the pale green packet back into the tiny ceramic container and pulled out the white sugar packet. "No idea but I'll bet it has something to do with the pumpkin contest."

"Oh really?"

"I mentioned her to you this morning. She and Beverly are the two main pumpkin growers." Lola's head tilted to show she was slightly miffed at me. "You don't absorb much do you?"

I shrugged. "Only when I find it fascinating."

I was facing away from the door, but I heard it open and shut. The familiar scent of coastal air came with it.

My lunch mate sat up a little straighter. "Speaking of fascinating. Don't turn around," she said quietly. (*I turned around . . . naturally.*)

Franki's latest customer was a tall, undeniably handsome man, thirty something and wearing a button down shirt, slacks and shiny black shoes. While his attire looked neat and proper there was just enough beard stubble to give him a slightly rakish look. His black hair was just long enough to curl up on the top of his no nonsense shirt collar. I hadn't finished taking catalogue of his attributes before I got caught in an accidental moment of locked gazes with the man. His brown eyes highlighted his rakish quality a bit. His mouth turned up in the slightest hint of a smile, or maybe it was just the way the light was pouring in through the diner windows.

I pulled my eyes away and turned back around. I picked up a napkin to fan the embarrassed blush from my cheeks. "I feel like I just got caught gawking over the senior class president in chemistry class." I breathed a sigh of relief when I heard the door to the diner open and shut.

Lola had a good laugh at my expense. "Don't worry. That's a normal reaction to Detective James Briggs. He just has that kind of confident, manliness about him that draws female attention. But he's a pretty plain-spoken, all business kind of man. I've heard rumor that his rather stiff personality is the result of a broken heart. He was married for a short time, but it didn't work out. He lives over in the next town of Chesterton. He's the lead detective for the entire stretch of coast that runs right through Port Danby."

"Fascinating," I said airily, even though I could still feel the warmth in my cheeks.

CHAPTER 5

There was just enough sunlight left for me to pedal my way home. With any luck and a good deal of energy, I'd be inside just as the early October sun disappeared behind the horizon. It had been a long week, and I was glad tomorrow was Sunday.

I hadn't realized how tired I was from the day of setting up shop until my bicycle hit the slight incline on Myrtle Place. Working in a big city had gotten me used to living without a car. Lack of public parking and a plethora of public transportation in the city made owning a car just a couple of unnecessary monthly bills. I'd purchased a small blue compact when I moved from the city to Port Danby, but the town was small enough that riding a bicycle was a perfectly wonderful way to get around. I was sure that would change in the winter when brisk winds and glacial rainstorms dropped in on the town, but for now, I was going to take advantage of the glorious autumn weather. And it helped me burn off Elsie's bakery samples.

Myrtle Place was the main road that ran parallel to Harbor Lane, but instead of forking off right to the coast and marina like Harbor Lane, it curved left and turned into Maple Hill. Maple Hill eventually ended at a tall, looming mansion that looked as if it had seen its better days many decades ago.

Myrtle Place, aptly named since it was lined on both sides by plush Crape Myrtle trees, also branched off into smaller neighborhood streets where most of the citizens of Port Danby lived in a mish mash of every style of house. My house, which I had purchased after I'd leased the shop, was on Loveland Terrace, the last small road before the Maple Hill turnoff. My small backyard afforded the perfect, unobstructed view of the dilapidated mansion on Maple Hill.

I pedaled past Graystone Church, and its accompanying rustic, little graveyard. Kingston had finally found his bird energy, and he soared along above me, stopping occasionally in the top of a Crape Myrtle just to annoy the smaller birds who were finding their evening perches.

With the exception of a few barking dogs and one particularly industrious ground squirrel, the streets were relatively quiet. I closed my eyes for just a second, took in a deep breath and wiggled my nose to see what people were cooking for dinner. Fried chicken mingled with somebody's curried lamb, making for an odd mix of odors. The unpalatable combination reminded me of my childhood, before I had the ability to regulate my hyperosmia.

Self-preservation had forced me to learn how to control my sense of smell. Growing up, I could hardly get through a meal, particularly if more than one aromatic food was on my plate. If I decided to peel a banana for a snack, and my mom was cooking an onion in the kitchen, then every bite of banana tasted like onion. In the third grade, I was so thin the other kids called me stick figure girl. My parents were worried sick. They eventually took me to a doctor who specialized in olfaction, the study of smell. Dr. Vickers showed me how to use my mind and other senses to control my sense of smell. She told me I was a superhero and that my super power was my sense of smell. That helped me regain some of the confidence I'd lost. My mom even sewed me a cape to play with at home that had the letters SN on it for Super Nose.

I passed Shire Lane, the last street before Loveland Terrace. My house was on the corner, so I could see it long before I reached my street. I could also hear my neighbor, who had this annoying habit of hammering and sawing things in the house from four o'clock until six. I had yet to see the mysteriously energetic and noisy neighbor. Whoever it was, they seemed to have a day job that left them only evenings for working on a house that sorely needed work.

Not that my small house was a shining star of the neighborhood. But it was cozy, and it looked lived in like a favorite pair of faded jeans. The pale yellow siding was sunny and welcoming, fringed as it was by a brown shake roof. My favorite exterior feature was a front porch that ran along the length of it. The white balustrades needed a good coat of paint, but I decided to go natural. I'd planted climbing pink roses around the base of the porch. With any luck and a not too brutal winter, the roses would be railing high by next spring's bloom. I'd lined the small front lawn with bluish green juniper shrubs. I planted deep green and ivory white wintercreeper for ground cover on the stretch of space between my lawn and the road. I thought it had all come together nicely.

The wavering shadow of my pet crow rolled over me as I turned my bike around the corner.

"Don't look now but I think you're being stalked by a crow," a deep, not altogether unpleasing voice called through the open window on the neighbor's house.

I squinted to get a look at the figure standing there, but the light was all wrong. I could only see my own house reflected off the top pane. I reached my driveway and as my front tire hit the ridge of cement, my keychain, house key and all, popped out of my bicycle basket.

Kingston, who had an affinity for shiny objects (*leading me to theorize that he was a pickpocket in a previous life*) swooped down and plucked the keychain up in his beak. He landed on the front edge of the roof, triumphantly holding the silver key in his beak.

"They do say crows are the smartest birds. I think this one wants you to invite him in."

I had no more time for my neighbor's remarks. I climbed off the bike. "Kingston, you come down here right now or you can skip dinner."

The crow came obediently down but without the keys. They clanked into the rain gutter.

I stared at the bird as he danced along the porch railing with his long talons.

"Well, you won't get dinner now anyhow. Neither will I, it seems." I walked up the porch steps, and out of silly desperation, I glanced through the transparent curtains on the front window to see if Nevermore was lounging nearby. Of course, even if he was, which he wasn't, it wasn't as if his cat paws could turn the lock.

I walked back to the front of the porch and held tightly to the front column that held up the left side of the portico. I climbed up on top of the railing with fingers crossed that it would hold my weight. I searched blindly in the rain gutter and crinkled my nose in distaste as my fingers grazed over wet mushy leaves and whatever else might have made its way into the gutter. Then luck. My fingertips grazed something metal. I plucked out the keychain. In my excitement, I'd forgotten that I was balancing on a four inch railing.

My arms spun through the air like worthless helicopter blades. I gasped in fear and shut my eyes to brace for the slamming pain that was sure to follow. There was some pain, but it was only slight, along with a short loss of wind. I opened my eyes slowly and found myself in a nice, big pair of arms.

The man took a deep breath of relief. "Didn't think I'd make it in time."

He stood there, his clumsy neighbor cradled in his arms, for a few seconds longer than necessary before lowering my feet to the ground. My eyes traveled up and stopped at his face. It was mid fall but his face and arms were tanned, which probably meant he worked at the marina. His thick blond hair went stunningly well with his green eyes.

"Are you all right?" he asked. "Aside from being stalked by a crow, that is."

"Everything is still in one piece. And he's not really a stalker. He's a pet." I smiled and nervously tucked my hair behind my ears until I silently reminded myself that I was twenty-eight and not twelve. And he was hardly the first handsome man I'd ever met. Although he was certainly the first to catch me as I fell off a porch railing. Unless, of course, I counted falling from an oak tree in fourth grade. But on that occasion, Stewart Germaine, my tall, skinny but semi-cute neighbor missed catching me, and I sprained my wrist.

The man stuck out a large and nicely callused hand. "I'm your neighbor, Dashwood Vanhouten, the third. But you can dispense with the long name and call me Dash."

"Oh wow, yes, that is a long name." He had a nice, strong grip. "I'm Lacey Pinkerton and you can call me Lacey or Pink. I answer to either." The house next door certainly didn't look as if it should belong to a man named Vanhouten or a man with the word 'third' following the distinguished surname. Maybe it was an investment. "If you don't mind me asking—where was the family fortune made?"

His smile was sort of Hollywood, big screen caliber. "What family fortune?"

"O—oh," I stuttered to find an appropriate way out of my social misstep.

Dash laughed and darn if it didn't just go nicely with the big screen smile. "That's all right. Everyone just assumes that a fortune came with the name. Which is exactly why my dad invented it. He changed his own name legally to Dashwood Vanhouten, the second because he thought it looked more distinguished on his office door than Darren Vooten."

I blinked up at him in confusion. "The second? I don't understand. If he made the name up, who was the first Dashwood Vanhouten?"

He shook his head. "There wasn't one. Dad just thought the second made him seem like part of an important family legacy."

I absorbed the name story for a few seconds and then laughed. "I haven't met the man, but I like him already." My stomach dropped in horror. "Oh my gosh, is he still alive? I just assumed again, a habit I obviously need to drop."

"No worries. Dashwood Vanhouten, the second is alive and well and living in Ohio."

Kingston cawed from the porch railing in a loud reminder about dinner.

"I should let my bird inside before he starts scaring all the neighbors."

"Right. And I think you have another pet waiting for you."

I followed the direction of his sparkling green gaze to the front window. Nevermore had his thick front paws on the windowsill, and his big head was pushing away the curtains.

"That's Nevermore, my gray tabby."

Dash's brow arched in question. "Nevermore?"

"Yes, I'm a big fan of Edgar Allen Poe."

Dash crossed his arms in thought and looked from the crow to the cat and back to me again. "But you have a big black crow, a raven of sorts. And you named the cat Nevermore?"

"Yes." I smiled. "Unlike the cat, the crow picked his own name. I used to live next to an elderly man who blasted out Kingston Trio records on an old, midcentury stereo console. Kingston loved the music, so I decided to name him after the band."

Dash nodded, but still looked a little confused. "Right. I guess I'll get back to my work." Before he took another step, he pointed back at Kingston. "How did you end up with a pet crow anyhow?"

"I found him near death after a big rainstorm and nursed him back to health. I sent him off to live in the wild again, but he showed up back at my door a week later."

"That's sweet. So he missed you then?"

"I like to think so, but I'm pretty sure he came back for my Belgian waffles. I'm pretty skilled with a waffle iron."

"Nice meeting you, Lacey," my handsome new neighbor said with a laugh before heading back to his house.

CHAPTER 6

*N*evermore licked every bit of food from his ceramic dish and stretched his gray striped paws forward for a good yawn. It was his 'catch y'all later' yawn before curling up on the sofa to finish his twenty-three hour cat nap.

Kingston had long since shut down for the night. I kept a dark sheet over his cage to keep him from waking me at the crack of dawn with an eardrum shattering good morning caw.

The moon was nearly full, and the sight of it, looking cheesy yellow out against the navy blue night sky, drew me out onto the porch. I had wisely grabbed a throw blanket to drop over my shoulders. It was definitely colder at night out on the coast. The usual shroud of nighttime fog was late, which allowed for a glorious view of the marina lights. Lola had explained that the Pickford Lighthouse rarely ran its light anymore because there were far more modern and efficient lighthouses and warning bells along the coast. But I'd seen the light circle through really heavy fog, casting an almost neon glow through the thick, briny moisture, and at least once, I'd been startled awake by the low, mournful howl of the fog horn.

A trail of three cars filled with laughing teens and blaring music came down from Maple Hill. It hadn't escaped my notice that an inordinate amount of cars traveled up a road that led nowhere except to a deserted old mansion.

"That old Hawksworth Manor is a favorite hangout for the kids." Dash's deep voice was already familiar to me.

I leaned forward and looked toward his yard. He was standing on the front lawn waiting for a large, shaggy dog to do his business. "This is Captain, by the way. But don't worry. He doesn't chase cats. No promises about the crow though because I have seen him dive helter skelter into a flock of resting seagulls."

I was surprised and not altogether disappointed to see my new neighbor again. He sat down on the porch step next to me. Captain lumbered over and flopped down at the bottom.

"What's the story behind that mansion?" I asked. "It looks as if it's been many years since anyone hung their hat there."

"You mean you still haven't heard the sordid tale of Hawksworth Manor?"

I looked up at him. "No but from the enthusiastic timbre of your voice, it seems I'm about to hear it."

"You are. But to do this right, I need to stand and have my silhouette in front of the moon." He pushed to his feet. "It was a hundred years ago today, give or take a few years . . . and months, for that matter."

"So, some time a long time ago?"

"Right. Anyhow, it was a rainy night and the sky was filled with thunder and lightning."

I squinted one eye. "Are you adding the creepy weather for effect?"

His broad shoulders dropped. "Was it that obvious?"

"Well, after the hundred years ago today thing I'm kind of taking the entire tale with a grain of salt."

Dash leaned his head back with a great, deep laugh that stirred Captain from his snore session for a brief second.

He caught his breath. "I'll just get to the good stuff. The Hawksworths were a rich family who owned this entire side of Port Danby. There was a husband and wife, Bertram and Jill, and three kids, all under the age of fifteen. They say it was a murder-suicide.

The only motive the police at that time could come up with was jealousy. But nothing solid was ever found to prove it. Apparently, old Bertram was convinced that Jill was having an affair with the gardener. In a fit of rage, he shot his wife and his three kids as they sat in the drawing room reading and playing cards. Then Bert turned the gun on himself and boom, one Hawksworth family wiped from the earth for good."

"Oh, that's awful. Those poor kids. Why does the town keep the old place standing? With that kind of history no one would ever want to live in it."

Dash sat back down. I allowed myself a quick assessment of his shampoo, soap and aftershave. All manly scents with a hint of spice. "You're right about that, but it's become a favorite destination for tourists and most especially ghost hunters. There's a gardener's shed in the backyard that has some of the gory pictures and other creepy artifacts on display. Tickets to look inside are five bucks and the money goes into the town coffers. That place might look like it popped up from some grim serial killer flick, but it's a gold mine for Port Danby."

"Wow, I can't believe this was the first I've heard about it. But then I have been terribly busy setting up shop."

"A flower shop right?"

"Yes, and I open in two weeks. I'm a little nervous about it, but I think that's just because I've never done anything quite like this before."

Dash stood up again. He was very . . . well . . . for lack of a better word . . . dashing, even draped in faded flannel and denim. "I think you'll do great. I'm glad you're here, Lacey. Sophisticated, smart, a good sense of humor *and* a pet crow. I think you're just what this town needed."

CHAPTER 7

I'd spent the entire Sunday being lazy and decided a little exercise wouldn't hurt. An early morning bike ride along Culpepper Road, past the bucolic landscape of family farms was just what I needed before another day of setting up shop. The east side of the road was lined with tall, frilly laurel hedges. They provided a brilliant green barrier wall. Strappy shrubs of red-hot poker intermingled with the hedges. Their signature fiery red and yellow spikes had long since withered with the long summer hours, but the spindly stems and leaves still stood proud and tall as they waited for the next bloom season. Patches of bold orange gaillardia, a long blooming plant that was still showing plenty of color, dotted the sides of the road in messy clusters.

The west side of the road was lined with quaint farms with rustic red barns and chickens pecking away at the insects in the pastures. One friendly looking homestead with a white farmhouse and cheery green chicken coop had a large hand painted sign leaning against a mailbox that was painted with black and white cow spots. I peddled to the west side of the road to read it.

"Fresh, organic eggs four dollars a dozen."

Perfect. Kingston loved hard boiled eggs. I had no place to store them in the shop, so I made a quick mental note to ride past the farm on my way home. Smartly, I'd added a handy basket to the front of my bike.

As I peddled past a street called Dawson Grove, a splash of orange caught my eye. I decided to take a little side trip along the road to admire the pumpkin patches. The first house I passed had a pumpkin patch that seemed to start right at the back porch. It stretched and sprawled across the yard and out into a pasture where several goats were grazing. A tall scarecrow was dressed, oddly enough, in a fireman's coat and helmet. I liked it. Some thin fencing had been erected around one particular pumpkin, a massive, deep orange squash. I concluded that it must have been one of the prize pumpkins being coddled and protected for the contest.

A thick border of purple and white lantana separated the two farms on Dawson Grove. I peddled past it to the next farm with its equally impressive pumpkin patch and even more impressive scarecrow. This scarecrow dawned a black top hat, frock coat and white cravat. Even Kingston, who normally thought nothing of scarecrows, might take a second look at the Mr. Darcy scarecrow. I'd been admiring the scarecrow and hadn't noticed the woman circling the patch. She was wearing a green linen apron and a blouse with pink flowers, a sweet elderly woman's gardening ensemble, only there was something not entirely sweet about her demeanor. She looked as upset as the woman hacking away at her steak in the diner. Her garden clogs were hitting the surrounding dirt so hard, a cloud of dust followed her.

"Morning," I said cheerily, hoping to add a little bright spot to her day. "I like your scarecrow."

Her straw hat shifted slightly as she glanced my direction. She grumbled something angrily under her breath and marched back toward her house. It seemed I'd met my first unfriendly local.

I decided my pumpkin patch detour had come to an end and turned my bike around to head back to Culpepper Road. As I rolled back past the patch and the finely dressed scarecrow, I noticed the name Kent was printed on the side of the parcel sized mailbox sitting atop a tilted post. I was sure Lola had mentioned the name Kent when she spoke of the pumpkin contest.

I glanced around the sky and surrounding trees for a familiar black bird, but Kingston had obviously decided to take his own route to work today. I wasn't quite ready to stand in the shop sorting vases by size and color, so I turned south on Culpepper and headed toward the beach.

The view of Pickford Lighthouse, with its powder white siding and shiny black cap, was by far the most idyllic in Port Danby. My only regret was that I couldn't see it from my shop. Still, on a clear day, if I took several steps down Harbor Lane and stood two feet north of the Port Danby Willy and then turned my body in just the right angle to see past the laurel hedge on Culpepper Road, I could get a slightly eclipsed postcard view of the squat little tower with its pointy black hat and big yellow light.

It was shaping up to be a brilliant blue day. I made the executive decision to explore the coast for a bit before heading into the shop. I could really get used to being my own boss.

The early morning air was still cold. I stopped to zip up my sweatshirt before returning my feet to the pedals.

CHAPTER 8

I rode my bike from Culpepper Road to Pickford Way. A sharp right turn rolled me right past Pickford Beach, the town square and motel row. The mayor's office sat quietly at the far west side of the town square.

Aside from a few men with metal detectors and a woman feeding the seagulls, the sand was empty. Beach days were behind us but that didn't stop weekend visitors from staying in town. I stopped at the vista where, with the right camera and skill, a person could take glorious pictures of the coastline. Gray granite rocks, layered with the occasional black shard of shale, made up the steep cliffs that dropped below the lighthouse.

I pedaled to the rather frail metal railing and peered over. A dizzy sensation struck me as I looked down the steep cliff, and I rolled my bike back from the edge. A small sign with red painted letters warned visitors not to climb over the railing or walk along the edge of the cliff. That was not going to be a problem for me. The outcroppings of rock below would not make for a pretty landing from any height.

I pulled my phone out to snap a picture of the lighthouse. My dad would get a kick out of it. Before I was born, he had spent four years in the navy. He had never lost that love of the sea and everything that went with it, including fishing.

I stared up at the squat white tower as it stood proudly on its green hillside. I had yet to meet the lighthouse keeper, but I'd heard he lived full time in the cottage that sat just beneath the lighthouse. The cottage's exterior matched the lighthouse with a powdery white coating of paint, but the sharply pitched roof was covered with brick red tile.

I took a few more pictures of the lighthouse from different angles. It was such a simple, plain structure, yet somehow, it transported me back to a more romantic time when salty merchant sailors and wild haired buccaneers traveled the seas in tall sailing ships.

A whistle shot up from the marina and carried clear over to the lighthouse. I turned my bike around and shaded my eyes to see where the sound had come from. It seemed I was once again going to meet up with my neighbor, Dash.

I rode back toward the marina. Just fifty years ago, the area had been a dock for industrial boats, but when the bigger ports nearby swallowed up Port Danby's business, the town rebuilt the coastline area and switched over to tourism as its main source of business. It had been a good choice. There was hardly a prettier, more welcoming stretch of coastline for a hundred miles.

A long set of parallel docks ran adjacent to the wharf, where stations had been set up to clean fish. There was a bike rental shop and a casual dining stop that proudly touted having the best shrimp salad in the world. A fishing pier, seafood shop and the shallow algae greased water that came with a marina could have easily overwhelmed my sense of smell if I allowed it.

My hands nearly popped off the handlebars when my tires hit the rough, stuttering planks of the dock. I turned along one of the short arms that branched out from the main dock. Most of the farther out slips were filled with recreational boats. The ones closer in to the fish cleaning stations were fishing boats.

Dash waved from the deck of what seemed to be an expensive pleasure boat. It was easy to distinguish because of the shiny lacquer hull and glossy teak deck. Whereas, the fishing boats tied off closer to the wharf, where pedestrians could walk and enjoy the world's best shrimp salad, looked like rusted tin cans in comparison.

Dash was wearing a tool belt, and the side of his right hand was covered in black grease.

I climbed off my bike and squinted up at him and realized he was pleasing to look at from every angle. "I thought there was no family fortune, and yet, here you stand on a fancy boat."

"Yes, and if only this fancy boat belonged to me. When I'm not hammering and annoying the heck out of my neighbors, I'm fixing boats. And actually earning money for my labor, unlike the work I'm doing at home."

"You must be Lacey, the Pink's Flowers girl," a voice sang out from a few boats down. A woman threw her leg over the side of a fishing boat and hopped down, rubber boots and all, onto the dock. She was a stout woman with cheeks round and red as apples. Her short yellow mackintosh coat creaked with each of her quick, long steps. Her jaw was moving wildly over a wad of tobacco or gum as she approached. I was relieved to see it was the latter. Spearmint, according to my nose.

She stuck out her hand. It was a strong grip . . . and icy. "Sorry about the cold hands." She rubbed them together. "I've been helping on the boat." Her fingernails grabbed her attention. "Oh, would you look at that." She gave me a close up view of the tiny palm trees someone had painstakingly painted onto her nails. "Lost a palm tree. Probably somewhere in the pile of fish guts I tossed out for the seagulls." The creatively painted nails did not match the rough and ready demeanor of the woman.

"I would imagine manicures don't last too long out here on the wharf. As you already mentioned, I'm Lacey, owner of the flower shop."

"Glad to meet you. I'm Theresa and that bald man with the long gray beard up at the bow is my husband, William. Though most people call him Willy."

I had been meeting enough people to make it hard to keep names straight, but Lola had talked about Willy and Theresa during her long narrative about the class ring.

"What brings you down to the dock this morning?" Theresa managed to chew the gum between every other word. She had the skill quite mastered, leading me to believe that she chewed gum a lot. It made my jaw tired watching her.

"I'm just out for a little exercise, but I need to get back to the shop."

"You should meet my husband first." Before I had a chance to respond, she yelled down the dock. "Will! Come meet the flower shop woman." There was no response. She gave it one more try and this time managed to alarm a row of pigeons off the railing of a nearby boat.

William's shiny head was now sporting a floppy hat. He leaned over the railing of his boat and waved hello, which was all the greeting I needed. It was hard to match the weathered, bearded little man with the image of somebody's high school sweetheart or secret flirt, but what did I know about love.

"Hey, Lacey," Dash called from behind. He was standing at the bow of the shiny luxury boat pointing up to a tall mast on the ship moored across the dock. "Isn't that your bird?"

I shaded my eyes and peered quickly up at the crow. "Yes, he's trying to remind me that I need to get to work."

I rolled my bike closer to the boat Dash was standing on. He leaned his forearms on the railing and smiled down at me. "Thought maybe he was looking for a *crow's nest.*"

"Clever man."

"Thanks. Been working on that one the last few minutes."

I pointed my thumb back behind my shoulder. "Well, I've got to get back to the shop."

"It looks good. Hope you don't mind but I was snooping in the windows while I ate one of Elsie's crumb cakes. I was going to sit at one of her tables, but she was busy rearranging them. She must have moved each table and chair a dozen times before I finished the last bite of crumb cake. She wasn't her usual cheery self. I'm thinking maybe she's been sampling the vanilla."

I sighed. "No, it's not the vanilla, but I think her mood is my fault. I wouldn't let her put the tables in front of my shop. Now, it seems, she's obsessing about them. I'd better get over there. I don't want her to be upset. Thanks for the tip off."

"Sure thing. Have a good day, neighbor."

"You too, Dash."

CHAPTER 9

I could hear the metal feet of a chair scraping cement long before I reached the little cluster of shops. Lester was inside the Coffee Hutch. His tables and chairs sat undisturbed in the morning sun. The front window of his shop was wide open, and, oddly enough, he had set a small fan on the ledge. It cranked and spun as it sent waves of rich coffee aroma out onto the street. I detected hints of almond in a medium roast scent.

Metal scraping on concrete pulled my attention to the neighbor on the opposite side. Elsie was wearing running shorts under her frilly apron as she leaned back to study her table arrangement. I parked my bike in front of the flower shop and walked over to her side.

Elsie heard me approach but didn't look up as she spoke. "I'm worried that the sun will be too bright for this end table after ten."

"I don't think it'll be a problem, but you could turn the chairs more to face the store. It's such a lovely shop." I hoped my compliment would produce a smile and it did. But it was hardly an exaggeration.

If ever a building could be described to resemble a cupcake it would be the Sugar and Spice Bakery. Elsie had had the building painted a butter yellow, the kind of color that made your mouth water even though it was slathered on bricks and plaster. The slightly arched front window was trimmed with candy stripes of teal and white. Billowy lace curtains provided a frilly frame for the shop's interior, which was equally charming. The same earthy teal paint was emblazoned across the letters spelling out the bakery's nursery rhyme name.

I walked over and put a hand on Elsie's shoulder. "Your customers line up for your delicious baked goods. Frankly, with treats like yours, most people would be happy sitting on a piece of crumpled wet newspaper on the sidewalk as long as they had one of your fudgy brownies clutched in their fingers."

"Thank you, Pink. And I haven't forgotten about your pumpkin bread. I've added in a nice ribbon of sweetened cream cheese. I think you'll like it. I've got some cooling right now."

"Perfect. I can't wait." I grabbed my keys from the bike basket and opened the door. The flutter of wings from behind reminded me to duck. Kingston swooped in and landed on his window perch. Seeing Kingston reminded me of my plan to ride home via Culpepper Road to pick up a dozen fresh eggs. If I still had energy after two long bike rides and a day setting up the shop, then I would throw together a frittata for dinner. Once I'd figured out how to control my hyperosmia, I'd found a renewed joy in food. I managed to stir, bake, burn and, occasionally, over salt my way to being a halfway decent cook.

I slipped into my tiny office space, which was really more of a closet, and checked my email. Featherton Nursery, a garden supply store in the neighboring town of Chesterton, had written to confirm the delivery of six flats of orange and yellow marigolds. When I spoke to the clerk on the phone, she mentioned that they had six flats of marigolds left over from summer, and surprisingly enough, they were still blooming. But since it was the end of the season for marigolds and these only had a few last breaths of color left, she offered them to me for half price. I decided a free potted marigold would be a perfect grand opening gift. I purchased small pink pots with Pink's Flowers printed around the side. It was my first real attempt at marketing, and I was rather pleased with myself.

I had not quite finished unpacking the multicolored vases I'd purchased for flower arrangements when Elsie hurried in with a small paper plate that was folding under the weight of a miniature loaf of pumpkin bread.

My acute sense of smell allowed me to taste things long before they reached my lips. Cinnamon, cloves and nutmeg did a little dance through my nose and down to the base of my throat. "I'm looking so forward to this, Elsie. I took a long bike ride this morning and I'm starved."

Elsie waited with bated breath as I took the first bite. A moist crumbly landslide of spicy brown sugar and pumpkin filled my mouth. "Hmm, even better than I expected and, trust me, I was expecting. And you're right, the ribbon of sweet cream cheese puts it over the top. Now I'm glad I took that bike ride because I plan to finish every bite of it."

Elsie looked pleased with herself, and it seemed the table arrangement issue had left her mind completely. "You should bring your running shoes. We could run the loop together some time."

I laughed. "No thanks. I think I'll spare myself *that* humiliation. Besides, you'd probably have to carry me home on your back."

I wasn't open for business but the door flew wide and my primitive alarm system of one rusty goat bell clanged through the shop. I'd seen Mayor Price before, but we'd never been formally introduced. It seemed that moment had arrived. His bushy moustache was not terribly symmetrical, and it twitched as he glanced around the shop. It seemed from the sour twist of his mouth, which was barely visible beneath the gray moustache, that he didn't approve of my taste. Which was not a bad thing considering the man was wearing a dark green polyester blend suit that was at least a size too small. I felt particularly sorry for the button that strained to stay shut over his big belly.

"Harlan," Elsie said enthusiastically, but a glower from the mayor caused her to abruptly change her greeting. "Of course, Mayor Price, how are you? Have you met Port Danby's newest citizen, Lacey Pinkerton? Isn't her shop beautiful?"

He grunted in response to her last question and stepped forward for a brief handshake. I put on my best smile. "Nice to meet you, Mayor Price."

The mayor nodded as if he were agreeing with the statement that it was nice to meet him. So far that was not the case, and when his nod was followed by a rather brazen survey of my face, I had to bite my tongue not to point out his rudeness. Maybe he just took some getting used to. He was, after all, a politician. Somewhere in our myriad of conversations, Lola had mentioned that Mayor Price was the fourth generation of Price in the mayor's office. She noted that it was mostly because no one else wanted the position.

Mayor Price leaned his head a bit and seemed to be focused on my nose.

Instinctively, I reached up to make sure it wasn't covered in the cinnamon streusel from Elsie's pumpkin bread. Everything seemed to be in order as far as my nose was concerned.

"Excuse me, Mayor Price, is there something on my face I should know about?"

"Uh, no." He straightened and pulled his focus away from my nose. "I was just trying to understand how you earned the moniker 'million dollar nose'. It looks like an ordinary nose to me."

Elsie laughed but cut it short when he scowled at her. "Why, Harlan, I mean Mayor Price, where on earth did you hear that?"

I looked at Elsie. "Apparently Mayor Price has been doing a little research on Port Danby's newest citizen." I raised my brow in question at him.

He fidgeted with the edges of his coat a second and then burbled out an excuse. "I take my job of keeping the citizens safe very seriously. You can never be too careful."

"Yes, of course," I said, trying not to let the sarcasm drip too heavily.

Kingston made a cooing sound, signaling that he wanted a piece of the pumpkin bread.

It took the mayor a good long moment and a pair of spectacles pulled from his coat pocket to convince himself he was looking at a crow. "What on earth is that?"

"That's Kingston, my pet crow." I begrudgingly broke off a piece of the pumpkin bread and walked it over to him. He plucked it from my fingertips and danced back and forth along his perch as he finished it. I gave a thumbs up to Elsie to let her know he'd enjoyed it.

Mayor Price's neck had darkened as if he was more than a little perturbed. Either that, or his collar was too tight, like the coat and shirt stretched around his belly. "I'm not entirely sure it's legal for you to have a wild animal inside a place of business."

It seemed my chance for a good first impression with the mayor was going south very quickly. But then, how much power could a small town mayor wield?

"Well, Mayor Price, until you can provide me with the exact ordinance number that states a pet bird is not allowed in a place of business, you can expect Kingston to be sitting in that window during business hours. Now, if you'll excuse me, I have a lot to do to get ready for my grand opening." I headed to the door, in case he didn't know where it was.

I began a sigh of relief as he seemed to take my hint but then sucked that air right back in when he stopped three feet from the door. "It seems rather strange for a woman to give up a six figure income in the city to start a flower shop in a small town."

I wasn't sure what he was getting at. His manner and suspicious tone seemed to have caught Elsie off guard too. She was, for once, quite speechless.

But I had learned early on how to speak up for myself. I stepped toward him. "Mayor Price," I said in a tone that left no doubt of where my words were heading. "I can assure you there is nothing untoward about a successful, creative woman seeking a change of scenery and career. Now, as I've said before, I have a great deal to accomplish before I open the door of Pink's Flowers. And once the doors are open, I think you'll find that I'm a hardworking, productive member of the town. Just like Elsie standing next to me."

He cleared his throat but didn't say anything else except 'good day, ladies' as he walked out. I took a few deep breaths to cool down before turning back to Elsie.

"You never mentioned that the mayor is, should I say, less than charming."

Elsie waved off his rude inquiry. "He just doesn't have enough to do. I'm sure once he gets to know you, he'll change his attitude. Although, I will warn you that he's pretty much a grumpy bear all of the time."

"I'll make note of that and avoid him."

Elsie pulled an orange ribbon off the counter. For no apparent reason, she tied her gray streaked hair up with it. "So is it true, Pink?"

"Is what true?"

"That they called you the million dollar nose?"

I smiled weakly. "I'm not really sure how it came to be. I think there was a rumor going around the perfume industry that Georgio Perfumery had taken out a million dollar insurance policy on my nose. It wasn't true of course, but one thing led to another and the next thing I knew I was the million dollar nose. Not exactly a girl's dream nickname."

"I think it's fabulous." Elsie walked over and checked her new hairdo out in the reflection of the front window. "My goodness, Les must be brewing extra strong coffee today. I can smell it clear through this window pane."

"I think it's because of the fan he set up in his front window. He's spreading the aroma out over the sidewalk." I went on with the explanation, not noticing Elsie's change in posture. Her thin shoulders were rigid like the arms of a clothes hanger.

She continued to stare out the window. "He's set up a fan, has he? That would explain why his tables are full. Well, we'll see about that." She marched out without saying good-bye.

CHAPTER 10

*A*fter the rough start with the mayor and a bit of a sidewalk war between Elsie and Lester, I had managed to get a respectable amount of work done. I locked up and headed out. My legs were tired from the morning ride, but I'd kept firm to my decision to stop for eggs. Since I'd also eaten a respectable amount of pumpkin bread to go along with the respectable day of work, I decided to take the longer more scenic route past the beach.

There was still plenty of sunlight so rather than fly toward home, Kingston decided to follow along as I rode down Pickford Way to Culpepper Road. A light fog seemed to be gathering along the coast line, signaling a chilly night at home. A hot frittata would be perfect.

The ride leading away from the coast on Culpepper Road was at a slight incline. I squeezed the rubber grips on my handlebars and stood to pump the bike along. Kingston flew on ahead. He swooped down over the verdant pastures and disturbed a few busy hens as they finished picking the grass clean of insects. In the distance, Maggie's wobbly mail truck turned the corner at Dawson Grove. The farm with the eggs was just past that corner.

Halfway up from the beach, Culpepper Road branched off into Highway 48. The highway was the shortest path to the neighboring town of Chesterton. Chesterton was about five times the size of Port Danby and with more stores and businesses. Whenever I couldn't find something in Port Danby, I headed to Chesterton. It was a far less charming town, and the stores and business district looked much more like a city.

I'd lost sight of Kingston and wondered if he'd gotten bored and decided to fly home. By the time I reached the egg farm, my heart rate was pounding at a pretty good clip from the uphill climb. I stopped in front of the sign to catch my breath. Just as I was about to climb off my bike and walk up to the door, a blood curdling scream cracked the quiet countryside.

My heart raced even faster as I hopped back on my bike and headed in the direction of the scream. By the time I rounded the corner onto Dawson Grove, poor, frightened Maggie was standing next to her mail truck, bracing her hand against it to keep from collapsing to her knees. Something terrible had frightened her so badly, her face was nearly as white as her truck. Her scream had been loud enough to send squirrels to their holes and chickens back to their coops, but no one had emerged from either of the two farmhouses on Dawson Grove to find out what was happening.

I, myself, was never one for remaining a useless bystander. Maggie, a forty something woman, who lived with her elderly parents just west of the town square, always wore a cheery smile as she delivered mail up and down Harbor Lane. She had been one of the first people to introduce herself when I arrived in town. But the usual cheer was gone, and she looked close to fainting.

I nearly jumped off while the bike was still moving. "Maggie, what is it?" I raced toward the truck. Maggie's shaky hand took hold of mine, but she couldn't speak.

"You should sit down."

Maggie shook her head and seemed to be edging toward a panic attack. She struggled to take deep breaths. At the same time, she was trying hard to get words out. When nothing came, she resorted to pointing. Her finger shook like it was rubber as she pointed in the direction of the pumpkin patch on the Kent farm.

"I think she's dead," she sputtered between shallow breaths. "I think she's dead."

I took her by the arm and walked her to the driver's seat. "Sit down." A crumpled brown lunch bag was wedged in next to the driver's seat. I reached over and grabbed it. I dumped the leftover bread crusts out of the bag and blew into it to open it up. "Here, Maggie, breathe into this while I go check things out."

I pulled my phone from my pocket and suddenly wondered if the same emergency number was used in Port Danby as in the big city. After all, the town was so small and interconnected, a person could almost stand on a porch with a megaphone to call for the police or an ambulance. I only hoped that neither was needed, and I would just find that someone had fainted or fallen asleep under a tree.

Those hopes were instantly dashed as the grim scene in front of me took shape.

I instantly recognized the pink flowered blouse, even hidden as it was by the large fingered leaves of the pumpkin vines. I hopped over the tangled stems and round squashes and quickly recounted all the steps and procedures for cardiopulmonary resuscitation. It had been a few years since medical school, but I was confident I could help.

I reached the woman and stumbled back a bit, not expecting such a horrid sight. The woman lay mostly face down with half her head inside a massive smashed pumpkin. I'd seen enough cadavers in medical school to feel quite certain that I was looking at a dead woman.

I dialed my phone and held it to my ear as I crouched down next to the woman. I pressed my fingers against her carotid artery and waited for some sign of life. There was none.

"Hello, yes, connect me to the Port Danby police department. And hurry please."

CHAPTER 11

t took me a few minutes to gather my wits after coming upon the horrible scene in the pumpkin patch. Some of the adrenaline had drained from my body, and my heart rate was adjusting to normal. While it seemed the entire scene was a tragic freak accident or heart attack, I decided not to touch anything.

I sat with Maggie at the mail truck. She, too, seemed to be catching her breath from the shock.

"I'm glad this was my last stop for the day," Maggie's voice was thin and shaky. "I don't think I could have finished otherwise."

I patted her back. "I'm sure the police will just ask a few questions and then help you get safely back to the post office."

Maggie's eyes and nose were red and puffy. She shook her head. "Poor Bev. And she was so excited about that giant pumpkin. Hers was the biggest this year. She was a shoe in for first prize." She sniffled once. "And now it seems that the pumpkin killed her. It looked like the thing was eating her head." She covered her face. It seemed it would be some time before Maggie wiped away the vision of Beverly lying dead in the patch with her head inside the pumpkin. It would be a while before I forgot it too.

"Maggie, does Bev have any family nearby? Next of kin, perhaps?"

Maggie shook her head. "I occasionally deliver letters and packages from someone named Susan Kent in Baltimore, a sister, maybe. Beverly and her husband had always wanted kids, but it never happened for them. And then Herbert died three years ago of heart failure. Poor thing has been alone ever since." Maggie reached for a tissue in her pocket and blew her nose. "Poor, poor Bev. She was looking so forward to the contest. She was sure she would win first place."

The plain car with the special plates that was always parked in front of the Port Danby Police Station pulled up to the farm with the black and white patrol car directly behind it. An ambulance with twirling red lights but no siren rolled around the corner and parked in front of the police cars.

The tall, lanky officer, who I'd seen drive past the shop in the squad car several times but who I had yet to meet, climbed out of his car. He straightened his gun belt with authority and pushed back his shoulders. He had a baby face. I doubted he was more than twenty-five. He also had a severe lack of chin and just a bit too much forehead. The few times I'd seen him I thought he looked a bit oafish. But it was entirely possible I had misjudged him.

Detective Briggs, who I so far only knew from the very brief glance exchange in the diner, got out of the car carrying a notepad. He seemed to be the smooth, cold cream to the young officer's hot coffee.

The young officer fidgeted again with his belt and stopped a good ten feet from the patch to view the body. "Everyone stand clear," he ordered in a loud, commanding voice even though Maggie and I were the only people included in 'everyone'. "This is officially a crime scene," he barked.

"No it's not," Detective Briggs quipped as he walked past the officer.

I now stood by my earlier oafish judgment.

The medics trudged across the dirt with their equipment boxes. A waste of effort, unfortunately. I decided to follow the detective into the patch.

He heard me trouncing through the leaves behind him and glanced back. "Are you the woman who called?"

"Yes, I am. She is quite dead, I assure you."

He looked a bit miffed that I'd already decided something that was better left to a pro. He crouched down and placed his fingers over the carotid artery. "As you said 'quite dead'."

He stood up and walked around the smashed pumpkin to get a view of it from all sides. The medics drew closer with their equipment. The detective glanced up from the grisly scene. "You can take that stuff back to the ambulance. We'll need the gurney after I examine the scene. I'm going to need you to take her to the morgue."

The detective looked around for what I could only assume was his second in command. The officer had not moved closer to the deceased. He busied himself, rather unnecessarily, drawing a dirt line around the patch with a stick. It seemed more than possible that he had not seen too many dead bodies in his young life. They looked decidedly more real in person than on a movie or television show.

"Officer Chinmoor," Detective Briggs said sternly.

The officer didn't look up from his task as he dragged the stick to the far end of the patch. "Officer Chinmoor," Detective Briggs said again a little louder. Something told me he was a man who rarely raised his voice and for that matter, rarely showed emotion. He'd walked onto the scene as if he was walking into a market for a quart of milk, as if finding a dead woman in a pumpkin patch happened every day. Which, from the nervous fidgeting of his partner, I could only assume was not true.

"Excuse me," I asked quietly. "Did you say Officer *Chinmoor*?" It was the completely wrong time and place to smile, but I had a hard time keeping my lips straight. I caught a flicker of amusement in the detective's eyes. Apparently, the irony of the name was not lost on him either. But he was losing his cool with the young man.

"Charlie," he snapped and finally got the officer's attention. His chin receded back even farther as he stared open mouthed at his boss. "I was just going to mark off the crime scene before I get the yellow caution tape."

"No, I need you to get the evidence camera. I need to get a few pictures before we move the body. And ask Maggie if Beverly had any friends or family that need to be called."

"Right." Officer Chinmoor was more than happy to pull himself away from the scene.

I, on the other hand, became more intrigued. I rounded the pumpkin and stooped down to get a closer look at her head. Orange stringy pumpkin goo was plastered across her forehead. I gently pressed my fingers around her skull.

I could feel an annoyed gaze raining down on me from above. "What are you doing?"

I stood up. "I don't feel any contusions or dents on her forehead."

"Well—" he stopped and looked at me. "Miss?"

I stuck out my hand but withdrew it when I saw it was covered in pumpkin slime. "Lacey Pinkerton. You can call me Lacey or some people call me Pink."

"I'll stick with Miss Pinkerton."

My shoulders drooped. "Right. Then I have no choice but to call you Detective Briggs."

"Yes, that's what I want you to call me." He wrote down my name, which I found slightly insulting because I rather hoped he would just remember it. But then, this was official business. "So, you were the first on the scene?"

"Well, no. That would be Maggie. She was delivering mail down Dawson Grove."

He scribbled notes as I spoke. "And where were you?"

"I had stopped at the egg farm for some fresh eggs. I was in the mood for a frittata. But I never got the eggs because I heard Maggie scream."

He looked around. "Then the bicycle belongs to you?"

"Yes. Now about her skull—don't you think there should be some sign of damage to her forehead if she actually smashed through the pumpkin? I mean, look how thick the shell is. That must be a hundred and fifty pound pumpkin. It was expected to win first prize."

He looked up from his notepad. "First prize?"

"The pumpkin contest?"

"Oh, right." It seemed the Port Danby Pumpkin Contest was of little interest to the man. "And you're right. The pumpkin shell is very thick for a human skull to break it."

I held back a tiny smile. "It also seems like she had to do quite a bit of contortion if she tripped and fell into it. It seems her hands would have at least been out to stop her, but they are both in strange positions." Beverly's left arm was beneath her. Only the fingertips were visible. Her right arm was relaxed and draped over her body as if she was just sleeping.

Officer Chinmoor returned with the camera. He stretched his arm out as far as it would go to hand the camera to Detective Briggs.

Briggs snatched it from his outstretched hand. "What are you doing, Chinmoor? Are you worried she's going to hop up and grab you? Go back to the squad car and call the morgue. Let them know to expect a body."

"Right." He scurried off, leaving a small trail of dust behind his shiny, regulation shoes.

Briggs shook his head.

"Your partner seems a bit squeamish about seeing a dead person," I noted.

"Yes, doesn't he? And he's not my partner." His dark brows were smooth and one arched up over his brown eyes. "I work alone."

"Of course. Although, I couldn't help but notice that while her skull seemed to be mostly intact, there's a small clump of blood at the back of her head."

Briggs walked around to get a look at the back of her head. He lifted the camera and took a picture. "Are you trained in forensics or criminal science, Miss Pinkerton?"

"No, not at all. However, I did attend two years of medical school before I had to give it up."

He crouched down for a few more pictures and then straightened. He was tall. Not quite as tall as Dash but then there were other qualities. Like the dark hair curled up on the shirt collar. I'd grown rather fascinated with that curl of hair.

"Why did you leave medical school? You seem well suited. As you might have noticed with Officer Chinmoor, not many people are comfortable around a dead body."

"It had to do with my acute sense of smell and the vaporous odors in anatomy lab. I kept passing out. The professors were sure I was just queasy. But it was the formaldehyde. No one else could detect it, but I was heady with it from the second I walked into the lab. It was for the best."

He nodded. "Well, I think I've got all I need from you, Miss Pinkerton. You should get home before it's too dark." As he spoke, he leaned down and took a picture of a dark red spot on Beverly's pink blouse.

"Is it blood?" I asked.

"Might be."

I leaned down, closed my eyes and wiggled my nose. When I opened them, I had an audience. Detective Briggs was watching me. "What are you doing?"

"Smelling the spot."

"From up there?"

"Yes, and you'll be interested to know it's not blood. It's ketchup." I took another whiff. "And something else, something that reminds me of pumpkin pie. Or maybe that's because I'm standing in a pumpkin patch. And then there was my overindulgence on Elsie's pumpkin bread."

His eyes widened, and, for just a second, he let go of his unflappable demeanor. "Elsie's making pumpkin bread?"

"With a sweet cream cheese ribbon running through the middle."

"Briggs," Officer Chinmoor called across the pumpkins, "I let the morgue know."

Briggs was right back to his more stiff self. "Right. Now get the tape measure. And hurry up. Also let Maggie know she can head home. She looked shaken. I'll talk to her tomorrow."

Briggs returned his attention to the blouse stain. "Ketchup?"

"Yes."

"So it's true. The million dollar nose? The crow?" He motioned with his head toward the fence along the road, where Kingston sat like a stone sentry watching over me.

"I guess the mayor stopped by the police station," I said.

"He did."

"And is the crow a problem?"

"Not for me but you might ask the finely dressed scarecrow. He doesn't look too pleased. Now, if you don't mind, Miss Pinkerton, I need to get back to work."

CHAPTER 12

The detective's somewhat blatant dismissal of me fell on deaf ears. There were numerous unanswered questions, which tended to make me curious to the point of driving myself batty.

With his very reluctant and slightly pale work partner, Detective Briggs measured out the placement of the body and set markers so Beverly could finally be wrested from her prize pumpkin. And it was that prize pumpkin that once again caught my attention.

The massive squash was sitting firmly in the ground a good three feet from the source of its ropey vine. I followed the vine to the center of the base plant. The thin fibers from the plant stuck to my skin as I parted several hand sized leaves. The vine was severed from the plant and not by the hand of nature. It was a clean cut. The pumpkin was no longer attached to its life giving roots. It seemed strange to think that Beverly would have cut the pumpkin from the plant with the contest still two weeks away. The pumpkin had probably reached its maximum girth, but if the contest was based at all on weight it might still have absorbed more moisture and therefore pounds. Or, at the very least, ounces.

I circled around the patch for clues but found nothing until I reached the garden gate. My foot accidentally kicked the edge of a garden tool. I brushed away some of the debris covering it and discovered a well maintained garden hoe. The green painted handle of the implement was still smooth and shiny, so it was either quite new or Beverly was one of those fastidious gardeners who took care not to leave her tools out in the sun or rain. Which made it equally strange to think that, either way, she would have left it out in the garden to be buried by soil and dead leaves.

I tore free a pumpkin leaf and used it like an oven mitt to lift the entire hoe free from its hiding place. Instantly, I smelled the acrid, metallic odor of blood. I turned the hoe to look at the sharp metal end, the edge used to cut hard dirt and break up thick loam. The pungent smell of soil mingled with the easy to distinguish smell of blood. The sticky looking lump on the corner of the hoe was a mixture of both.

"Detective Briggs," I called.

They had freed Beverly from the pumpkin. She was stretched out onto her back. "Miss Pinkerton, I thought you were going home." There was a bit of aggravation in his tone but then he was helping to move a rather hefty dead woman.

"It's just that I've found something that I think you'll want to see. It's not ketchup."

The confusion in his brow lasted only a second and then it dawned on him. He said something to the medics and headed over to where I was standing with the hoe. I pointed to the sticky wad at the end of the tool. "Blood."

"You're certain?" He took a whiff. "I smell soil and fertilizer."

"Yes, that too, but there's blood mixed in."

"Right." Before he turned to get an evidence tag, he stopped to look at me, giving me and my nose the same once over that Mayor Price had done. Only Briggs did it with much more finesse and somehow I didn't mind.

"It's just a tiny button of a nose with a few freckles. How on earth could it be so powerful?"

I smiled. "The shape and, most assuredly, the freckles have nothing to do with its power."

He turned to walk away. "Uh, Detective Briggs? The hoe?" I held it out to him.

He nodded in approval at my use of the leaf to avoid confusing possible fingerprints. He took hold of it, carefully placing his fingers between mine on the leaf.

"This changes everything, doesn't it?" I asked, silently chiding myself for getting excited about the possibility of a murder mystery. A woman had died after all. But still a tremor of giddiness rushed through me.

"It might. We have to make sure the blood wasn't from an animal. Mrs. Kent might have used it to club a gopher or rat to death." His face popped up. "Unless you can tell the difference with that super nose of yours."

"No, I can't. It makes sense that it might belong to an animal. Although, there is that blood on the back of Beverly's head."

Detective Briggs smiled faintly. "Go home, Miss Pinkerton and leave the police business to the police."

"Yes, I will." Eventually, I thought wryly as I watched him return to the body. I walked to the gate. Sawdust had been strewn around the fence surrounding the garden. I walked out of the gate and crouched down. There was definitely something besides pine shavings lingering in the air. I closed my eyes and took a deep breath. I still couldn't make it out, but it was something familiar and pungent. It would, of course, drive me crazy for the rest of the evening, so I pinched some of the sawdust between my fingers and took another whiff. Lantana. There were few ground covers as strong smelling as lantana.

The faint odor of lantana sparked something in my mind. There was a thick border of it stretched between Beverly's farm and the neighbor's.

I decided to head that direction. Kingston's shadow coasted over me. I'd forgotten all about him. He landed on the fence and shook out his feathers.

"Kingston, go home." I motioned toward Myrtle Place with my arm. He paced the edge of the fence a moment and then lifted his big wings and took off.

The ambulance rolled past with Beverly Kent inside. Briggs mentioned there would be an autopsy as early as tomorrow to find out how she died. It sure seemed as if he, too, was thinking along the lines of a possible murder.

My own intuition was running right along those lines as well.

And Mom thought I'd get bored in Port Danby.

CHAPTER 13

The sun was just starting to drop lower in the sky, which meant I still had a bit of time to explore.

I reached the lantana border between the neighboring farms, not completely sure what I was looking for. Possibly a flattened footprint trail running through the plants. Someone, probably even Beverly herself, had recently tromped to the pumpkin patch with lantana flower smashed on their shoes. It was a thickly planted border that was quite overgrown but easy enough to cross with some high, careful steps. It had obviously been there for a long time.

Lantana grew with long, weedy stems, and the tiny blooms were fairly hardy. Usually it took a heavy frost to kill them off. And even then, they came back quite readily. The purple and white border was deep.

I was so preoccupied looking for possible footprints in the plants that I failed to notice I was being watched until the sound of a throat clearing carried my attention to the neighboring farmhouse. The woman was mostly hidden by the white columns supporting the portico jutting out over her front porch, but I could see the edges of her dress as they fluttered in the breeze.

There wasn't much to stop me when I was in a curious mood. And

I was definitely that. I hopped over the lantana border and headed across the yard and past the scarecrow clad in fireman's gear. The giant pumpkin being guarded by frail fencing sat stoutly in the late afternoon sun soaking up the last remnants of photosynthesis for the day. Unless it too had been severed from its vine.

I made a quick note of the fact that this pumpkin was not nearly as big as the one next door. It was absurd to think a woman had been murdered because of a pumpkin but then human nature was often absurd. I was anxious to know if this pumpkin had been cut too, but as I glimpsed the woman standing in the shadows of her porch, I saw that she looked quite shaken. And familiar. It was Virginia, the woman I saw at the diner the day before carving her steak with fury.

Naturally, she would be shaken. The activity next store made it obvious something dreadful had happened to her neighbor. And yet, she hadn't made the trip across the yard to find out. It was entirely possible she was too frightened to walk over. She looked properly horrified, as anyone might if their neighbor had just been carried off on a gurney.

I stopped for a moment to catch my breath and find my words. It seemed my insatiable curiosity had just landed me in the unfortunate position of bad news breaker. With any luck, she had already figured out the worst. It seemed so from the lack of color in her face and the way she braced her hand on the column for support.

I placed my foot on the first step and waited to see if she would ask me to leave or get off her property. Instead, her lips quivered a few seconds and she blurted out a question. "Is she dead? Is Beverly dead?"

"I'm afraid so."

Her eyes closed and she swayed. I raced up the remaining steps and caught hold of her arm. "Let's get you inside for a glass of water."

She nodded weakly and allowed me to lead her into the house. A small, outdated but charmingly rustic kitchen sat off what would have been considered the parlor back in the day the house was built. Two orange striped cats were stretched out on a faded floral sofa. They hardly lifted their heads as we walked through. The house smelled of dust and animal dander. I wiggled my nose to keep from sneezing.

Virginia sat at the round kitchen table, and I opened a few cupboards to find a glass.

"I can't believe it. Was it a heart attack?" Virginia had recovered a bit faster than I expected. Her words were far less shaky. "She told me she'd been taking some nitro—nitro—something or other for her heart."

I filled the glass and placed it in front of her.

"Nitroglycerin pills? They are quite common, but I'm not sure how she died. Detective Briggs says there will be an autopsy."

Her face had regained some color. One eye was slightly clouded by a cataract but her surprise was clear. "I thought I saw Detective Briggs there. Why would he be there? It couldn't have been anything but a heart attack," she insisted. "Bev was overweight and then there were those pills. And I don't think those pills were such a good idea. That stuff explodes, you know?"

"Well, the pills don't explode, but I'm sure, like you say, it was a heart attack." She was getting worked up. I decided it was not my place to put ideas of murder and intrigue in her head. Although, if it was murder, Virginia had a motive, flimsy and shallow as it seemed. But people had been murdered for less.

A dog scratched at the door in the service porch off the side of the kitchen.

"That's Spunker. He'll want his dinner." Virginia pressed her hands on the table to get up and let him in.

"No, let me." I hopped up first and walked to the screen door. Spunker didn't even give the stranger standing in the service porch a second glance as he pranced through with a good amount of mud on his paws.

"Oh, Spunker, have you been playing in the pig pen again?" Virginia's tone was airy. Apparently, the shock had already worn off. "Taylor must have left the gate open."

I glanced around the service porch as she continued her light-hearted scolding of her dog. There was a deep basin sink that was filled with several dirt covered root vegetables, two turnips and a big red beet. A clothesline ran from one end of the tiny room to the other.

A wire basket was bolted to the wall behind the clothesline. It was filled with various seed packets. One packet that was pressed haphazardly against the wires of the basket caught my eye because, unlike the commercially prepared packets of tomatoes and beets behind it, the label had been printed and taped on. The words Pumpkin Giant Hybrid 17 were written in bold print across the label. The corner of the packet was torn off. It looked flat as if there were no plump pumpkin seeds inside.

I swung around. A rooster print garden apron hung on a hook. A pair of garden shears hung on the next hook. I took a closer look at the piece of greenery jammed between its blades. One quick whiff confirmed what I already knew. It was the vine and leaf of a pumpkin plant. The odor was still quite fresh. Virginia was recently pruning vines and leaves in a pumpkin patch. Someone wanting to grow a massive pumpkin might very well prune back various vines to send all the plant's energy to one squash, but it was a little late in the growing season for that. Virginia's patch did reach her front porch. It was possible she had to cut some rogue vines from the steps to keep from tripping on them. Pumpkin vines did tend to get out of control when given unlimited space.

Virginia had busied herself filling Spunker's food bowl. I decided to take the opportunity to lift up her garden clogs and give them a once over with the *million dollar nose*. I'd always joked with my coworkers that I needed to buy some designer handkerchiefs because a regular tissue just didn't seem appropriate.

It was always harder to find one particular scent in a scrambled mix of odors, and Virginia's shoes were a veritable *salad* of farm smells. Manure, grass, crushed leaves and even pine from sawdust clung to her shoes in a big gluey mess.

I closed my eyes and twitched my nose a few times. There it was. It was faint and mostly drowned out by the pungent smell of manure, but Virginia's garden clogs had recently walked through lantana.

"Excuse me, dear, but why are you holding my garden shoes?"

I had been concentrating on the smells and hadn't heard Virginia approach. "Oh, I was just admiring them." That was, of course, a lie.

"I'm planning to start a flower garden in my backyard. It will help cut down on overhead costs for the store." That part was not a lie. Thankfully I had a slice of real life to add to the lie to make it sound more plausible.

She seemed to buy it. "Yes, those are very comfortable. I can give you the company name if you'd like."

Virginia reached for a recipe box on the shelf where her laundry soap was stored. Her fingers were still slightly shaky but that might just have been from advanced age. She fished through the recipe box and pulled out a small scrap of paper. "Garden Gnomes and Clogs." She held the paper out. Ten minutes earlier she'd looked close to collapsing from shock about her neighbor's death. Now she was going about her day, chastising her dog and handing out information about garden shoes. It was odd.

I waved off the paper. "Perfect. I'll remember that name. Since you're feeling better, I'll head home. It's been quite an afternoon."

"Yes, I suppose so. I'm sure it's no easy task opening up a shop for business."

"Actually, I meant the dreadful discovery of your neighbor, but yes it isn't easy opening a shop."

Her face grew slightly gray upon mention of her neighbor. "Yes. I can't believe she's gone. We've been neighbors for decades. Our husbands were friends." She made no mention of her friendship with Beverly. Perhaps she thought it was implied.

She walked me to the front door. As she opened it, we were both slightly stunned to see a tall figure standing on the other side.

"Miss Pinkerton," Detective Briggs said with a slight edge of impatience. "I thought you went home."

"Yes, well, I'm still here."

"So I see."

CHAPTER 14

Detective Briggs stayed out on the porch. It took him a second to pull his gaze from me as he spoke to Virginia. "Mrs. Hopkins, I wonder if I could talk to you for a moment." He made no move to walk inside, so Virginia stepped outside.

My mind was still buzzing with so many details and questions, I decided to make one more sweep of that service porch. I patted the pockets of my jeans. "Oh my, I think I might have dropped my house key in your kitchen or service porch. I'll be right back."

Detective Briggs had the most nicely shaped and expressive eyebrows. At that moment, his brows were questioning my motives. I winked at him and slipped back inside to the kitchen.

The detective's deep voice rumbled out on the porch, but I couldn't make out the words. The somber tone led me to believe he was talking to her about Beverly's death.

Spunker had finished his supper. He looked up with surprise as I scurried back through the kitchen. He trotted behind me into the service porch and watched as I snooped around. Thank goodness animals couldn't talk. The seed basket and the hand labeled packet of seeds grabbed my attention again. It seemed the pumpkin patch wasn't just the unlikely setting for Beverly's tragic death. My instincts, which were sometimes remarkably sharp, told me that the pumpkins played a role in all of it.

I leaned back to get a glimpse of the front door. I could see Virginia's chestnut and gray hair over the top of the window curtains. She was still talking to Briggs.

I grabbed the basket off the shelf and reached for the pumpkin packet. I smoothed my fingers over the thick paper. It was empty. I took a closer look at the label. Featherton Hybrid Seeds was printed across the bottom in a tiny font. Featherton was the name of the nursery in Chesterton. In fact, they were delivering some marigolds to the shop in the morning.

I'd spent long enough looking for my imaginary dropped key. Besides, I was more than a little interested in the conversation outside on the porch. And there was one more thing I needed to ask Virginia about, something she had, of all things, told Spunker. Because even if they can't talk, we humans spend plenty of time talking to them as if they could.

Detective Briggs looked up from his rather solemn expression as I stepped out onto the porch.

"Did you find it?" he asked me, temporarily pulling away from his conversation with Virginia.

I blinked at him. "Find what?"

His head tilted just slightly. "The key?"

"Oh yes, right. Just remembered, it's in the basket on my bike."

"Thought it might be." Smooth and plain-spoken as he was, he was not terribly skilled at hiding sarcasm.

I glanced over at Virginia and saw that she was clutching a tissue. Her eyes and nose were red. Interesting. It was almost as if she had just learned that her neighbor was dead, instead of hearing it twenty minutes ago from me.

"I'll get out of your way. Take care, Mrs. Hopkins, and again, I'm so sorry about Beverly." I tilted my head toward the yard as I walked past Detective Briggs, but he didn't catch on to my discrete head motion.

"Mrs. Hopkins, you've had a great shock," Briggs said as I

descended the steps, slowly, in case something of note was said on the porch behind me.

"Yes, I think I'll go inside and rest my aching head," Virginia said.

"Oh, Mrs. Hopkins," I called back up to the porch. Detective Briggs turned around and waited for me to continue. Sometimes he worked so hard to keep an official, stern face it made the tiny muscle in his jaw twitch. (*I hoped I wasn't causing it.*)

"Would you like me to close the pig pen? You mentioned that you thought Taylor left it open when Spunker came in with muddy paws."

"No, don't worry about that." There was the slightest hint of a chortle, but Virginia swallowed it back quickly. After all, her neighbor had just died. "That pig is far too lazy to wander out from his pen."

"Of course. Is that Franki Rumple's son, Taylor, you're talking about? One of the twins?"

"Yes. He comes over to fix things that are broken around the farm. He's not the ideal handyman, but he's all I can afford."

"Miss Pinkerton," Detective Briggs said sharply. "The sun is setting. You should get on your way if you're riding a bicycle."

"You are absolutely right. But Detective Briggs, if you have a moment, I just needed to ask you something about city ordinances."

He seemed to be assessing whether or not I actually had a city ordinance question. Which I didn't. "Isn't it something that can wait?" he asked.

I shook my head once. "No, it's a very pressing matter. I'll just wait out by my bicycle until you're finished with your conversation. And, if you don't mind, Mrs. Hopkins, I'm going to wander through your patch and admire your pumpkins."

"Absolutely, dear, and thank you for helping me inside."

I skirted around the pumpkins and headed straight to the center piece, the carefully guarded pumpkin in the middle. Virginia Hopkins certainly had the overall demeanor of a sweet, elderly woman. It was almost ludicrous to imagine her doing anything as sinister as killing her neighbor. I reached the biggest pumpkin. A long curly vine snaked out of its stem. I followed it with my eyes to the source plant. Just as I'd expected. Virginia's pumpkin was still firmly attached to the plant.

CHAPTER 15

I pulled my sweatshirt out of the basket on my bicycle and zipped it on. The sun had dropped low enough that the cool ocean air swept onto shore. Out on the horizon, a tall cluster of billowy white clouds signaled that Port Danby would wake to heavy fog.

Detective Briggs was still scratching notes on his pad of paper as he spoke to Virginia. She seemed to crumple a little more with each question. Sometimes I wish I had super hearing to go along with my super sense of smell. It would have been nice to hear what was being discussed.

I looked across at Beverly's pumpkin patch. A small sparrow was sitting on Mr. Darcy-crow's top hat. Officer Chinmoor had haphazardly draped yellow caution tape around the area where Beverly's body had been discovered. The remnants of the broken squash sat as a grim reminder of how the poor woman ended up face first in her prize pumpkin.

I looked in the direction of Myrtle Place and didn't see any sign of my crow. Hopefully, he'd made it to the porch. Not that I worried about Kingston as much as I worried about the havoc he might cause on his way home. Aside from occasionally terrorizing smaller wild birds and even the unsuspecting cat, Kingston was just a little too comfortable around humans. He had been known to swoop down and join people at their backyard barbecues and park picnics. On one disastrous occasion, he even landed on a woman's large straw hat. The woman ran around screaming something about Alfred Hitchcock and the birds. In Kingston's defense, the hat was decorated with yellow baubles that looked like cooked egg yolks. Something told me the woman never wore that hat again, which, in a fashion sense, was probably for the best.

Detective Briggs walked down the steps as Virginia slipped inside. Briggs had a surefooted way of walking that let you know he was a man of integrity. And he had a pretty broad set of shoulders to go with that self-assured stride. He surveyed the pumpkin patch as he walked past.

I was nearly bursting with information to tell him. He seemed to sense that. For a moment, I thought he was going to stroll right past me or just wave and tell me to go home. But he rounded the driveway post and the mailbox and walked over to where I stood with my bicycle.

"Does this have a light? It's getting toward dusk. That is the hardest time to see cyclists on the side of the road."

"I'll be very careful. I'm just heading to Loveland Terrace."

"Ah, Loveland Terrace. Right by the old Hawksworth Manor. Then you should be wary of teens driving past on their way to the mansion. They like to head up there and hang out."

"Yes, I've noticed. I have yet to visit the place, but I must say, the whole murder-suicide story is intriguing. When I finally have a free moment, I'm going to read up about it."

"So you're interested in murder mysteries?"

"You noticed? I did a lot of reading as a kid. Agatha Christie, Sherlock Holmes, the Hardy Boys. My nose might be considered special, but I can tell you as a kid who couldn't eat a piece of toast while smelling day old chicken in the trash can, it was anything but special. I was so skinny, I didn't have many friends. I think the other kids thought I was sick." I hadn't told the story for empathy, but there was a genuine hint of it in his face. Whenever the serious detective veneer broke away for a second, it gave a glimpse into his real character. And I liked what I saw.

"How did you learn to control it?" he asked.

"It took some time and working with experts who knew all about hyperosmia."

"Hyperos—never heard of it."

"It's a heightened sense of smell. I guess I've taught you something today. "

"I guess you have." He pushed his pad of paper into his pocket. "But it seems a heightened sense of smell is an understatement."

"Thanks. I think. Speaking of that. I took the liberty of snooping around the crime scene."

He smiled and shook his head. "Not yet. Let's wait for the autopsy."

I pointed at him. "But you think it might become a crime scene, don't you?"

He slid his chin back and forth. It seemed he was considering whether or not to answer. The black beard stubble I'd noticed in the diner was heavier and darker. But then it was getting close to evening, so that made sense.

"It might be a crime scene. There are some things that don't look quite right. The bloody lump on the back of her head," he added before I could. "It's just hard to understand why someone like Beverly Kent would be the target for homicide."

I looked toward Virginia's house. I caught a glimpse of her standing in her front window. She disappeared quickly. "I've heard that the pumpkin contest is quite a big deal in town."

His laugh was short and dry. "Yes but then everything is a big deal here in Port Danby."

"Did you happen to notice that Beverly's prize pumpkin had been cut from its vine?"

He looked over toward the yellow tape and then back at me. "I didn't. But I don't see how that matters."

"It's just that the contest isn't for two weeks, and the pumpkin could still—"

"—grow, but not if it was cut off." He finished for me. "You're right. I'll keep that in mind."

"Virginia's pumpkin is still attached. In case you were wondering. Oh, and I smelled lantana on the sawdust around Beverly's patch."

He looked slightly confused.

I waved my hand at the long stretch of lantana. "It has a very distinctive odor, and it separates the two farms."

There were two lines that creased next to his mouth when he grinned. "Just as it would be hard to understand a motive for killing Beverly, it would be equally hard to picture Virginia stalking her neighbor with a garden hoe. But, again, I'll make note of the pumpkin plants."

I made a point of looking at his shirt pocket where he'd slipped his notepad. An audible sigh followed as he pulled it free.

I stretched my neck and glanced at his pad. "You have very nice writing for a man," I noted.

His grin tried to break free again, but he kept it hidden. "Anything else, Miss Pinkerton? Pinkerton," he repeated. "Any relation to the famous Pinkerton detective of the nineteenth century?"

"Don't I wish. No relation to Allan Pinkerton, unfortunately. But I understand my great-great grandfather, Norville Pinkerton, invented a pair of socks with reinforced toes. But then he lost the toes in an accident and didn't need the socks after all."

This time he couldn't hold back the grin. He clicked the pen closed. "I'll let you get on your way before it's too dark. Thank you for your help today."

"My pleasure." I climbed onto the bicycle.

"Where's the crow?"

"Hopefully waiting for me on the front porch. I'm sure we'll see each other again, Detective Briggs."

"I'm sure. Oh, and Miss Pinkerton, leave the police work to us."

"I will try but I can't always help what this nose does." I tapped the side of my nose. "It sort of has a mind of its own."

CHAPTER 16

The layer of clammy fog was so pervasive, it seemed to seep beneath the doors of my house. I decided to wait it out for an hour or so, figuring it wouldn't be wise to ride a bicycle in a pea soup mist. Drivers would have a hard enough time as it was. The last thing they needed was to be watching out for a silly woman on her bicycle. I could have taken my car, but I'd grown fond of riding around town on two wheels. It gave me a certain sense of freedom, something I never had in the busy, traffic choked city where a simple bike ride was basically attempted suicide.

Nevermore danced around my legs, wrapping his long, striped tail around my jeans as he did his seductive 'feed me' routine. I held my breath and forked the chunky bits of meat into his bowl. Cat food was one of those smells that could overwhelm me and make me nauseous if I didn't take precautions. I had finally found the one cat food that filled two necessities, least smelly for me and best tasting for Nevermore.

I washed up, poured myself a cup of coffee and stepped out onto the front porch. One thing I loved about fog, and a coastal fog most of all, was that it always carried remnants of the earth and sea with it.

This morning's was particularly briny as if it had hovered out over the ocean for a long time before coasting in to blanket the town. I closed my eyes and searched for hints of linen from sails, fuel from boats and the salty odor from the crowded tide pools nestled in the rocks below the cliffs.

"Hey, neighbor," Dash called from the sidewalk, breaking me from my thoughts. Captain was plodding along next to him on wide, fuzzy paws. The dog had a jaunty blue scarf tied around his thick neck. Dash stopped at the foot of his driveway and held out his arms. "Beautiful day, isn't it?"

I laughed. "I suppose we have entirely different definitions of beautiful."

"That's because you work inside and I work outside. I love the sun, but it sure can be a bother when you're out working in it."

"Ah, I see your point."

"Well, have a nice day." His Hollywood caliber smile followed. Nutty woman that I was, I immediately made a quick mental contrast between my *dashing* neighbor and the more severe and far more serious detective. I had no idea why my mind went that direction, but it certainly did.

Dash walked inside with Captain, and I went back into the house for my heavier sweatshirt. I had a bit of time before I needed to get to the shop and decided to use that time for a quick stroll up Maple Hill to Hawksworth Manor. After all, could there be any better time to visit the scene of a grisly murder than an eerie, gloom filled morning?

Kingston was not happy when I made him stay behind, but even with stark black feathers, he was far too hard to keep track of in a heavy fog. I pulled the hood of my sweatshirt up over my head of dark blonde hair. It tended to curl into Shirley Temple style tendrils in damp air, a look I'd fought with every form of hot hair torture implement in my teens. Now I just let nature take its course. It was amusing how things you were obsessed with as a self-conscious teen, faded easily into oblivion once you were well into adulthood. I had actually hated my full bow shaped lips as a young girl, and I worked hard to minimize their impact by drawing them in whenever I felt a boy was looking at my lips. Eventually, I discovered where boys and men were concerned, they were an asset and not a flaw.

I strolled out onto the sidewalk and turned in the direction of Maple Hill. Since the Hawksworth Manor was the only building on the hill and since it had been built long ago, the white sidewalk ended abruptly and a gravelly path lined the curved incline leading up to the manor.

The house was truly a gothic masterpiece, complete with two pointy turrets mostly stripped of their green roof shingles. Multiple stories with steeply pitched gable roofs sat in between the turrets. Dark, dusty window panes stretched across the front. More than one window opening was covered with plywood, signaling that the leaded pane had long since been broken. With the mist so heavy, I could only see the tops of the bulbous cement balustrades running across a balcony that acted as the roof over the front porch. In its glory days, and before its occupants were brutally murdered, the house must have been quite a grand sight sitting up on its lush green hill. Now it almost looked sorrowful from neglect.

Unfortunately, the historical grandeur of the place was slightly ruined by the hastily constructed chain link fence the town had propped up around the exterior of the house. Multiple warning signs were posted around the fencing. But my intuition, and the multiple soda cans and beer bottles strewn around the foundation of the house, assured me those warning signs were mostly ignored. A five foot chain link was hardly an effective barrier for thrill seeking teenagers or ghost hunting tourists. Or overly curious flower shop owners.

The fog didn't just provide spooky atmosphere, it provided me with the perfect cloak. I walked to a set of bricks that some clever trespasser had set up to easily climb the fence. I put my feet on the bricks and carefully climbed over. Another smart thinking person had set bricks on the other side. The bricks wobbled some as I stepped on them.

Patches of grass and weeds lined the path leading up to the wide front steps. I looked back toward the road and discovered that, even through the gray mist, there was an incredible view of the entire town and coastline from the top step. The early morning sun had made some headway with the fog, but a dark gray mass of clouds still hovered above the ocean. In the distance, gulls screeched in annoyance about the bad weather over the water. How marvelous it must have been for the Hawksworths to stand out on their porch with their cups of hot tea and coffee and gaze down at the picturesque view. But how sad that their grand life came to an abrupt, bloody end.

The most I'd hoped for with my clandestine climb over the fence was a dust covered squint through a window or two. I walked to the magnificent stately front doors. They were at least twelve feet tall with ornately arched tops. Two lion face door knockers stared down at me with metal hoops hanging from their patina covered fangs.

Just for fun, I stepped back in time and lifted the ring to give the door a knock. As I visualized myself standing in a crinoline bustle and whalebone corset waiting for one of the servants to greet me, the massive door creaked open. I stepped back quickly, worried that a guard or possibly even a thief was inside. But the only thing that ushered out was the stale, musty odor of century old dust and mold.

I hesitated but for only a brief second. I had an opportunity to look inside a piece of Port Danby history, and I wasn't going to waste it. I promised myself I wouldn't go too far inside, and I'd stay off of rickety stairs. It would be terribly embarrassing to have to be pried out of a collapsed staircase inside a house that was clearly marked *do not enter*. I could only imagine the snide remarks and grins Detective Briggs would produce on such a discovery.

As I predicted, the long staircase leading up to the second story landing looked unstable and treacherous. A few of the steps were collapsed into splintered heaps, leading me to deduce that previous trespassers had not been as cautious. With the dust on the windows and the fog outside, the entryway was as dark as a windowless closet. I truly hated the dark. It wasn't a fear so much as a phobia.

I hurried through the lightless entryway and caught only a glimpse of a grime covered chandelier hanging down from the vaulted ceiling above. At one point in time, it must have lit up the entryway, the stairway and the entire second story landing. Now it was just a crystal draped dust collector.

I crept into a short hallway that opened into a cavernous room where most of the ceiling tiles had littered the splintered wood floor. Even though the entry and exterior had lost every shred of paint, the room off the entry still had green paneling between the ornate ceiling molding and base boards. Most of it was peeling off in strips that reminded me of the peel of a cucumber. A broken down piano that was void of most of its keys sat in the darkest corner of the room. I wondered briefly if I was standing in the room where the children were playing cards and reading when their father shot them.

I ventured a few steps farther into the room, and a bone deep shiver went through me. I blamed it on the cold air seeping in through the windows and holey roof. I walked toward the piano, but a creaking sound behind one of the wall panels sent me quickly from the room. There was no telling how many wild animals had decided to make their homes in the nooks and corners of the old house.

The coastal breeze that would eventually carry off the fog had begun to blow outside. Even though it was a fairly light gust of air, it managed to shake the windows and eroded, frail walls of the home. A sharp howl of wind circled the house once, and the door to the piano parlor snapped shut behind me. I gasped, not just from the sudden sound, but because with the door shut, the window light was gone. I was standing in the center of the pitch dark entry, with only the occasional tinkling sound of the overhead chandelier to drown out my short panicked breaths. My heart pounded. I quickly had to stop my active imagination from dreaming up all manner of creatures that might be lurking in the dark behind me. I felt my way to the massive front doors and was relieved when my hand brushed against the brass door knob. I turned it quickly and pulled. Briefly, it felt as if I'd pulled the door open. But there was no light or fresh air. I was holding the antique door knob in my hand. I reached for the second knob, but it was frozen in place.

"Oh darn, darn darn." The blackness began to close in on me. I sucked in a long, steadying breath and promptly dissolved into full panic. I grabbed the frozen door knob and shook it wildly. "Hello, is anyone out there? Help! Anyone. I'm stuck inside!"

The racing heart that had plagued me seconds before moved steadily to my ears so I could hear my own pulse. It pounded in my head like loud footsteps.

I made a fist and hit the door several times. "Please!" A noise in the darkness startled me. I spun around wildly as if I would be able to see something, anything in the blasted entryway. All I could see was darkness and shadows that were even darker than the dark.

I turned back around and pounded the door again. "Help!"

Suddenly, the door without the knob pushed open. I stumbled back and fell hard on my bottom. After standing in the dark, it took me a second to be able to see the tall figure standing in the open doorway. Especially with the light of day shining behind him.

"Well, if it isn't my spunky, tenacious neighbor." Dash stepped inside and lowered his hand for me to take. "Sorry, I guess I should have planned that better. I knew the door opened inwardly but didn't take into account the thoroughly terrified woman standing behind it."

He pulled me to my feet.

"Not thoroughly terrified. Just mildly panicked." I brushed the back of my jeans off, sending a respectable cloud of dust into the air. We both waved our hands in front of our faces to clear it away.

"How did you know I was here? And thank you, by the way. I'm pretty sure there's a pack of rabid animals living in these walls, and they were already breaking out the recipe book to see how best to cook me." I motioned toward the door. "Let's go before they pull out a second pot for you."

We walked outside. I was relieved to see that glorious sunlight had begun to paint the sky blue. "So how did you know I was here?"

"I was putting stuff in my truck. I saw you heading up to Maple Hill, and I thought, I'll just bet Lacey is going up to Hawksworth Manor. And then I thought, she's just the type of person to ignore the warning signs and climb right over that fence."

"I see. I guess I did exactly that. You seem to be a good judge of character."

"It depends on the character. C'mon adventure woman, I'll give you a ride down in the truck."

CHAPTER 17

here was a cluster of people in front of Elsie's bakery as I rounded the corner of Harbor Lane. I didn't need that super power hearing to know what they were talking about. The drawn faces and stunned expressions confirmed my guess. News of Beverly's death had obviously reached town.

Elsie came out of the shop the second I parked my bicycle. "Oh, Pink, is it true? You discovered poor Beverly dead in her pumpkin patch?" She didn't give me a chance to answer before she hugged me, filling my nose with the smell of cinnamon and vanilla. "How horrifying that must have been for you."

"In truth, it was Maggie who came upon her first. She was quite shaken by it all."

Lester came around the corner with a cup of tea for his sister. "Here, Elsie, drink this. It'll help calm your nerves."

Elsie took the tea and breathed in the scented steam. Lemon, honey and black tea I surmised from the fragrance floating off the cup. She sipped the hot beverage and then sighed as if it had provided instant relief. "Thank you, Les. You're a dear." Elsie turned to me. "Is it true she fell head first into her prize pumpkin? What a terrible way to die."

"Well, I think we'll know more after the autopsy."

"An autopsy?" Lester asked. "I suppose that makes sense when the cause of death isn't clear."

Elsie sputtered her tea back into the cup. "Come now. Not clear? What else could it have been? She was taking pills for her heart. She should have exercised more." Elsie shook her head. "She and Virginia always took the pumpkin contest far too seriously. Why, Beverly would be talking about it as early as March. Virginia too. And they'd both hardly be talking to each other by the day of the contest. It was ridiculous, and I've told them both as much. And now look what happened. Bev stressed herself right into a heart attack." Her phone alarm went off in her apron pocket. "Oh, my cupcakes are done."

Lester watched his sister hurry away with the cup of tea. "I suppose I'll tell James Briggs to just turn in his badge. He doesn't need to do any investigation at all. Elsie, the baker, has already summed up exactly what happened. Even added in some of her usual unwanted advice." When Lester smiled it forced his cheeks up into two round balls.

His mention of Detective Briggs piqued my attention. "Do you know Detective Briggs well?"

"Little Jimmy Briggs?" He touched my arm and lowered his head. "Don't tell him I called him that. I used to work in the Chesterton fire house with his dad. Jim's a smart guy and a good detective."

"Yes, he is. And very serious," I added for no real reason.

"How are you doing then, Lacey? It must have been a shock to find a dead body."

"I suppose it should have been, but don't forget, I attended medical school. It's a terrible tragedy though. Poor woman."

Lester nodded. Being a retired fireman, he knew how easily death could take someone.

A white box truck circled the corner of Harbor Lane. "I think this might be my marigolds. I better open the shop."

"Right. Where's Kingston? I haven't seen him staring down from the plum trees this morning."

"I went on a walk this morning, (*I had no intention of bringing up my adventure in the mansion*) and he was so mad that I left him behind, he refused to come along with me to work. It's just as well. I have a lot to do."

The white box truck pulled up in front of my store. A young man with a thick cap of black hair climbed out carrying a clipboard. "Lacey Pinkerton?" he asked.

"That's me."

"I've brought you some marigolds."

"Perfect." I walked to the door and unlocked it. "I'll see you later, Les." I waved as he headed back to the Coffee Hutch.

The man carried in my six flats of marigolds. A few were already wilting, but I couldn't complain. It was late in the season, and I'd gotten them for a great price.

The young man, whose nametag said Kyle, filled something out on the clipboard and handed it to me for a signature. Featherton's Nursery was printed in bold green type across the top.

"Do you work for Featherton's Nursery?" I asked as I signed the paper.

"I'm an independent trucker," he said proudly. "I make deliveries for businesses all along the coast. Daryl Featherton is one of my regular clients."

I handed him back the clipboard. "I'm new in town, so I haven't met Mr. Featherton yet. But since I'm running a flower shop, I'm sure I'll get to know him well." I doubted a young, freelance delivery man would know much about the businesses he worked for, but I decided it wouldn't hurt to do a little digging. "I've heard Mr. Featherton grows and nurtures hybrid seeds." Of course, all my information was based solely on the ripped open packet in Virginia's wire basket.

Kyle looked around at the shop. "Looks nice in here."

"Thank you."

"Uh, yeah. He has some botany degree or something, and he likes to experiment with different seeds. He grew a fruit that was half fig and half apple once, but it was pretty disgusting. I think he landed some contract with a big seed company though. But that's only from pieces of information I hear when I'm at the nursery." He ripped off my copy of the receipt and handed it to me with a gracious smile. "Have a good day."

"Yes, you too."

CHAPTER 18

$\mathcal{A}$fter a busy morning organizing things for the store opening, my back was tired and my stomach was empty. My unsettling start to the day, getting trapped in a dark house, had left me too frazzled to make a lunch. I was regretting that now. I was also feeling a little lonely without Kingston gurgling and chirruping from his perch. I decided to walk across the street and see what Lola had planned for lunch.

I locked up. The sidewalks had quieted down after the morning rush of neighbors and shop owners lamenting the sad news about Beverly. I hadn't seen Lola for a day. I knew her parents had shipped a large crate from Italy, and she had been busy cataloguing and pricing the newly arrived antiques. I'd asked Lola once why she didn't sometimes travel with her parents. It sure sounded exciting to me to traipse around the world looking for long lost treasures of history. Lola had responded with a short, terse laugh and muttered something about how *exciting* and her *parents* didn't go well together. I'd left it at that. It wasn't as if I spent much time with my own parents anymore. (*Mental note—call Mom.*)

Lola had decided to change out the string of jingle bells on the door for one of the goat bells. She said she liked how confident the bell sounded when the door opened.

"Hello," I called out and was answered back with a cuss word.

"Ouch, ouch, ouch." Lola popped up from behind a tall crate wearing an old Led Zeppelin t-shirt and sucking her fingertip.

"Uh oh, did I cause that?" I walked to her counter and pulled a tissue from the box.

She wrapped the tissue around her finger. "No, it was the darn staple on the crate." She gave the wooden crate a light kick. She waved her hand at the piles of sawdust on the floor. "Apparently my parents found the most remote section of Italy where they have not heard of bubble wrap and cardboard."

I walked over to the items she had pulled from the crate. An old iron with a grate for hot coals was sitting next to a sizeable lighter that was shaped like a suit of armor. The fuse was on the top of the helmet. Sitting beside the prettiest pair of green enamel candlesticks was an oil lamp with a handle and a long spout. It was heavily engraved with a pattern. I picked the lamp up and gave it a rub. "Do you think there's a genie inside?"

"Already tried. It's just a lamp. But now I'm going to have to write a sign for it that says 'please don't rub the lamp'."

I rested my hand on the top of a butter churn. The handle of the churn had been worn smooth from time and use. "I'll bet a lot of butter has been made in this thing."

"Speaking of butter—are you hungry?"

I smiled. "That was my main purpose for walking over here." I pointed at her tissue covered finger. "That, and of course, coming to see if you needed any first aid."

"Let me just wash up. I think Tom and Gigi have some fresh sandwiches made up at the market. How does that sound?" Lola asked as she walked to the restroom.

"That sounds great."

She turned on the sink but kept up the conversation. Her voice echoed off the bathroom wall as she spoke. "I heard you were the one to find Beverly head first in her pumpkin."

"Not entirely true." I sat on the stool behind the counter. "Maggie saw her first."

Lola came around the corner still drying her hands. The bleeding had stopped. "What were you doing on Dawson Grove?"

"I rode home that way to buy eggs for a frittata, which I never got to make. I ended up eating two pieces of cinnamon toast for dinner. Not exactly a buttery, cheesy frittata. Wow, now I'm really hungry."

Lola grabbed her closed sign and her sweater. "I'm ready."

"Something just occurred to me," I said as we stepped outside. "I saw Beverly earlier in the day, before I went back to get the eggs. I should have mentioned it to Detective Briggs. I guess I was so caught up in the shock of it all, I forgot to tell him."

Lola's face had snapped my direction with the mention of Detective Briggs. "You spent the shocking afternoon helping Detective Briggs? Lucky you. Well, I don't mean the part about the dead body. But you know. Why do you think it would have been important to mention to him?"

"It's probably not. I mean it was just a brief exchange. Not really an exchange at all. I had noticed she was stomping around her patch looking a little put off by something, so I decided a cheery greeting was just what she needed. She muttered something angrily back at me. Apparently, she wasn't as sweet and friendly as she looked. William chose the right woman. Theresa is much more charming."

"Beverly Kent?" Lola said with round eyes. "She's the sweetest woman ever. At Christmas she makes a massive batch of rocky road fudge and delivers it to all the shop owners." Lola's face dropped. "Or at least she used to. You must have caught her at a bad time."

"I must have." I didn't say any more about it but decided I would let Detective Briggs know just in case.

CHAPTER 19

The Corner Market was situated on the corner of Harbor Lane and Pickford Way, the last shop before the harbor and the beach. White lacquer paint was made to look even whiter by the four periwinkle blue awnings covering the four front windows. Someone had taken the time to hand paint navy blue and silver stars below the front window. A pretty, whimsical touch that made it look more like a magic shop than a corner market. A group of high school kids were standing inside and around the front of the shop snacking on potato chips, snack cakes and all the other goodies you learn not to eat in health class.

Lola's steps grew heavy. "Ugh, looks like bad timing. The high school kids must have had a short day today. Hopefully there are still some good sandwiches."

"If you look at the food in their hands, it seems they breezed past the sandwich shelf and went straight to the junk food. Which is exactly what I would have done at that age. I guess mother nature gives you more common sense about nutrition once you pass twenty. Otherwise, we humans probably wouldn't have survived the invention of processed food."

Lola sighed loudly and said 'excuse me' with equal vigor as she waited for two girls who were too busy gazing at something on their phones to clear the doorway. They laughed at something on the screen and then scooted out of the way.

As Lola opened the door, one of Franki's twin boys walked out with a smiling girl holding his hand. Franki's kids were all tall and attractive. Her boys always had that just stepped out of the surf look with their perpetual tans and sun-bleached hair. Seeing him reminded me of Virginia and the pig pen. I had to quickly trace back to the conversation to remember if it was Taylor or Tyler. Taylor, I thought. I decided it would be my only chance to ask a few questions.

Lola looked back to see if I was following. "I'll be right there, Lola." I followed the two teens. "Excuse me, Taylor."

He turned around. "I'm Tyler." I wondered just how many millions of times in his short life he'd had to utter those same two words.

"Oh, right, sorry. I should have known by the—" I swept my hand around my own face and my hair trying to find something that was unique to Tyler, but there wasn't anything. They were as identical as two people could get.

He was already bored with me. "Taylor is over there." He pointed down the sidewalk.

"Great, then I'll just catch up to him. And sorry again about the mix up."

He shrugged his shoulders. "I'm used to it."

I picked up my pace to catch up to Taylor, who was walking with several friends. "Excuse me, Taylor." I reached him.

He turned around and was surprised and no doubt disappointed to find that I was the person calling him instead of one of his school mates. His friends were equally disappointed, and they continued on. "I'm sorry to stop you on your way to wherever you're heading, but I was just wondering if you were at Virginia's house at all yet today. I was wondering how she was doing." It was my lead in question for what I hoped would be an easy segue into my real question.

"I've been at school," he said curtly and then seemed to think better of being impolite. "Sorry, that sounded harsh." Franki didn't have it easy, but she was doing a good job raising so many kids on her own.

"I'm sure she's upset. She and Beverly always fought a lot, but they were kind of there for each other. They drank coffee together almost every morning."

"What a shame Virginia lost her friend. So they fought a lot? Did you hear them fighting yesterday?"

"I was only there for an hour feeding animals. But it always gets kind of tense between them when the pumpkin contest gets close. Virginia thought she was going to win this year with the special seeds and all. But every time she pulled out her binoculars to check out Bev's patch, she got red in the face. Bev had a monstrous big pumpkin this year." His attention was pulled away by some laughter farther down the sidewalk. It was his brother and several girls. It seemed he was anxious to join them.

"I won't keep you from your friends any longer, Tyler."

"Taylor," he corrected and pointed ahead. "Tyler."

"Right. Sorry."

I hurried back to the market, sure that Lola was going to be mad I deserted her. I walked inside. Most of the kids had cleared out. With no small amount of organization and planning the owners, Tom and Gigi Upton, had managed to fit three stores worth of goods into their tiny space. Every counter, shelf and corner had its purpose. Chrome metal tables of varying sizes were spilling over and piled high with breads, fruit and energy bars. Even the ceiling was filled with Mylar balloons, baskets and ropes of garlic. A long row of glass fronted refrigeration units glowing with fluorescent lights took up an entire wall. On a hot day, it was the only cool place in the store. It was where I found Lola still trying to decide between tuna and ham.

She looked rightfully annoyed when I reached right past her to grab the last turkey and cheese.

"I'm standing here agonizing about which sandwich to pick and you walk in and grab the turkey without a second blink. Maybe I wanted the last turkey."

I held it out, but she shook her head. "Nah, I'm going for the ham." She reached in and grabbed the sandwich. She'd been holding the door to the refrigerator section open for so long every glass panel was fogged up. We each grabbed a bottle of lemon flavored tea from the open cooler and headed to the counter.

"It's nice out," I noted. "Maybe we should eat these in the town square."

"I've got time. Sometimes that shop closes in on me."

Gigi Upton was a pleasant forty-something who'd moved to Port Danby with her husband Tom ten years ago. They were unable to have kids and decided to make a big move and life change, much like me. (*Except I hadn't tried the kid thing yet.*) They did have two adorable dachshunds named Molly and Buddy, and Gigi was big into dressing them up. Today Buddy was sporting a dapper yellow sweater as he came around the counter for a greeting.

Lola pet him while I paid for my sandwich. Gigi had sparkling green eyes and a friendly smile. But her smile faded quickly. "Just terrible to hear about Beverly. Still can't believe it."

"Yes, very sad. Has there been any mention of a funeral? I know she didn't have much family in the vicinity."

Gigi handed me back my change. "I've heard she has a sister on the east coast, but I don't know much more than that. Herbert is buried at the cemetery at Graystone, so I'm sure Beverly will be too." Gigi was visibly distraught as she spoke. "We'll miss her around here."

"Yes, I've no doubt of that."

Lola paid for her lunch and we headed toward Pickford Way. The town square was more of an oblong hexagon. There were some nice mulberry trees for shade and several picnic benches sat around the perimeter. A massive three tiered fountain sat smack dab in the middle of the town square, but I had yet to see it run with water.

Lola and I found a table that was far from the road and from the fish smell coming off the wharf. That way I could actually taste my turkey sandwich.

My mind had been preoccupied with Beverly's death, and I hadn't taken note of the other people eating lunch just a table away.

"Yoo hoo, Lola and Lacey, how are you? Lovely day, isn't it?" Theresa's sing song voice chirruped through the air.

We waved back. Lola gave me a stiff brow lift. "Guess she's a happy camper now that Beverly is gone." She took a surreptitious peek at their table. "And just look at poor Willy picking at the bread on his sandwich. He looks like the boy who just lost his puppy, shoulders all slumped and jowls drooping like a hound dog. Not Theresa though."

Lola was right. William's posture was crumpled and his head looked too heavy for his neck. Whereas Theresa was talking animatedly about something. Her hands, fancy nails and all, were fluttering around describing something to her husband, who had absolutely no interest in the topic. But that didn't seem to faze her at all.

"It's true." I picked open my sandwich package. "It looks as if they are sitting at two different tables instead of right across from each other. She looks like the yin to his yang." I smiled at my fun analogy, but it earned a look of confusion from my lunch partner. "Never mind. But I will say, I met Theresa yesterday, and she was quite gregarious. Came right over and introduced herself. Maybe she isn't the kind of person to get sour or down about things." I decided to give Theresa the benefit of the doubt, but Lola was not going along with it.

A short laugh popped from her mouth, and she quickly covered it with a napkin. "Theresa? No way. She's one of the moodiest, quick to anger people I know. She can be bubbly and friendly one moment, but if you accidentally spill a tiny bit of hot mocha latte on her arm while you're reaching for a stirrer, then watch out because the Dr. Jekyll side comes out."

I swallowed the bite I was working on. "Since there were so many specifics in that example, I'm going to assume that you spilled coffee on the woman and a tirade followed. But I think you mean Mr. Hyde."

Lola's brow's squeezed into one long question. I enjoyed spending time with Lola, but occasionally I wished she were just a touch more worldly.

"Mr. Hyde? Dr. Jekyll was the thoughtful, intelligent side of the monster. Although, he did seem to know what he was doing when he drank the tonic. Anyhow, unless spilling hot coffee on Theresa's arm made her more thoughtful, then I think you mean Mr. Hyde."

"Yep, that's who I meant." She scooted closer as though the trees and pigeons might be listening in on our chat. "Did I tell you I signed up on one of those dating sites?"

"Did you? A reputable one, I hope."

She pulled the dill pickle out of her sandwich package and swung it around. "You bet. It's called perverts, serial killers and creeps dot com."

"Very funny. Just be careful. There are a lot of nutty people out there." I looked back toward Harbor Lane. The detective's car was parked out front of the police station. "I think I'll stop in to see Detective Briggs on our way back. I want to let him know about how upset Beverly was in the morning."

"Of course." Lola managed to make a simple nod seem condescending. "You should tell him. It's funny how me bringing up a dating site took your mind right over to the handsome Detective Briggs."

"Nothing funny about it. I have important information for him."

"Uh huh, very important," she said as she took another bite of sandwich.

CHAPTER 20

While most of the shops in town had their own unique welcoming style and each multicolored facade added to the town's eclectic charm, the Port Danby Police Station was sort of nondescript and dull. Of course, it wasn't a shop and it wasn't meant to lure customers in from the sidewalk.

I walked through the tinted front door, with its crooked, vinyl shade pulled halfway down to keep out a blast of sunlight. There was a chin high counter that ran the length of the front room. A metal gate separated the counter into two big sections. In a rather sad attempt to be festive, someone had taken the time to tape a few paper jack-o'-lanterns to the front of the counter.

Officer Chinmoor's mound of black hair was visible just above the counter. He looked up to see who had walked inside.

He stood and nodded. "How can I help you, ma'am?" Ugh, I was a ma 'am. When did I become a ma 'am? It seemed he suddenly recognized me. "You're the woman who found Beverly Kent in the pumpkin patch." He put up his hand to stop me, so he could pull my name up from memory. "Miss Pinkerton, the flower shop owner."

"Yes, that's me. I was wondering if I could talk to—" Before I could finish, the office door opened and Detective Briggs walked out.

Instantly, the vision of 'little Jimmy Briggs' popped into my head, and I had to hold back a smile.

"Miss Pinkerton, hello."

"Hello, Detective Briggs. I was just walking back from lunch at the town square, and I remembered there were a few things I wanted to mention about yesterday."

"That's fine. We can talk in my office. Officer Chinmoor, buzz her in." A loud buzzer sounded and the metal gate popped open. I walked through and into the office.

He left the door ajar and circled behind his desk to sit down. There was a manila file folder on his desk with the name Beverly Kent typed on the label.

Briggs motioned toward a chair. "Please sit. I have news back from the coroner that might interest you."

I sat down in the stiff metal chair and tried to look relaxed. Somehow, the combination of the man across from me and the unforgiving hard chair made that impossible.

Briggs opened the file. "Now, I need you to keep this quiet. This town works up enough rumors and fanciful stories on its own. They don't need any help with that. I just thought with your medical background, and—" He stopped and looked up at me with just a hint of a grin. "Your highly curious mind," he added. "It seems Beverly died from a blow to the back of the head. I've sent the hoe in for analysis and fingerprints. But the coroner said the injury to the back of her head looked consistent with the edge of something hard. So, well done on that."

I shifted on my seat, feeling pretty pleased with myself. "Thank you. Since it seems this has turned toward a homicide investigation, assuming Beverly did not hit herself with the garden hoe, I should let you know that I saw Beverly the morning of her death. It was early. Maybe seven. She was quite distraught about something. She was pacing around her pumpkins muttering angrily to herself. It might be that she came out to discover that her pumpkin had been severed from its vine."

Briggs wrote something down in the folder. "Thank you. Now, if there's nothing else, I'm on my way to Chesterton. I had a look around her truck and found a piece of notepaper that had two phone numbers on it. They belong to a garden nursery and a farm supply store, both in Chesterton. I need to retrace her steps from yesterday. I'm going to head out there after I finish up some paperwork."

I sat up at the word nursery. "Featherton Nursery?"

He pulled his notepad out of his shirt pocket and looked at it. "Yes, that's the one. It hasn't been there long. When I was a kid, the lot was used for weekend yard sales and Christmas trees in winter." He put the notepad back into his pocket and stood to see me out.

I got up to leave but decided since I had his undivided attention, I'd ask him one more question. "Detective Briggs, have your read much about the Hawksworth murders?" I would have brought up my little morning adventure if it hadn't been illegal and, well, embarrassing.

"I've dabbled in some of the history. There's quite a collection of information about it in the library. And I suppose if someone gave it a lot of time and effort, someone with a highly curious mind," he added, with a pointed look "—could figure out what really happened."

Now he had my undivided attention. "What really happened? Do you mean it wasn't a murder-suicide over an affair?"

I liked the way those lines appeared next to his mouth when he was amused. "I'll leave that for you to discover. The library is just a mile out on Highway 48. But be careful. The bike lane is narrow along that stretch of asphalt."

"I will and thank you. Now I've got a mystery to solve, and I do love a good mystery." I was just about out the door when it occurred to me I'd been had. I turned back to face him. "And that's exactly what you were hoping for, wasn't it, Detective Briggs? Distract the silly flower shop owner with a century old murder so she'll stay away from the Beverly Kent case."

He didn't even try to hide it. "As I've said, you should leave police business to the police. And, for what it's worth—" he paused. "I don't think you're the least bit silly, Miss Pinkerton."

"Well, thank you. That's reassuring. Good day, Detective Briggs."

"Good day, Miss Pinkerton."

CHAPTER 21

I'd left the police station and had not gone more than a few feet before deciding that I would take a bike ride out to Chesterton. I had every intention of following up on the detective's suggestion that I check out the library to read about the Hawksworth murder. But not today.

After learning that Beverly had died from being hit on the head, my mind was shooting off like fireworks. Who could have done it? And why? Did her frail, elderly neighbor and pumpkin growing nemesis club her with a garden hoe? The fact that Beverly's prize pumpkin had been destroyed at the same time left a lot of open questions. The lantana smell on Virginia's shoes, the pumpkin debris jammed in her gardening shears and then of course the motive all pointed toward Virginia. Could a pumpkin contest have actually driven a perfectly sweet woman to murder? And then there was overly cheery Theresa. She seemed to be one of the few long time inhabitants of Port Danby who wasn't the least bit affected by news of the death. And poor William certainly looked devastated. An extra-marital affair was always a solid motive for a murder of passion.

I reached my shop and grabbed my bicycle. Lester waved to me through his front window as I rode past. I had no time to chat. The ride to Chesterton would take at least thirty minutes and if it got too late, I wouldn't be back before dark. By then, my pets would be more than ready for dinner.

I decided the shortest route was to ride toward the coast and take Pickford Way across to Culpepper Road. From there it was only a mile until the turnoff for Highway 48. Although to call it a highway was rather a stretch. It was really just a nicely paved ribbon of asphalt, divided into two lanes with a wide border on one side for bikes and pedestrians. If time permitted, I planned to stop at both the nursery and the farm supply store. I wasn't sure what I would do once I got to those places, but something would come to me. My curiosity and deductive reasoning skills were both working in high gear.

I pedaled past the town square and caught a quick glimpse of Mayor McGrumpy walking down the steps outside his office. He watched me as I rode by. No waves were exchanged. It seemed the man would have preferred if I'd stayed in the city with my million dollar nose.

There was a nice downhill as I hit Culpepper Road, but that ended abruptly as I turned onto the highway. My basket wobbled back and forth as I gripped the handlebars and stood up to pedal. Several cars rode past me at a much higher speed than I expected. I was thankful for the bike lane.

I continued on my way, listing in my head all the things I wanted to ask Featherton about his seeds. My flower shop gave me the perfect reason to inquire about his seeds and plants.

I heard a car come up behind me and braced for the burst of wind and tiny grit storm as it flew past. Instead, it slowed. I stared straight ahead, not wanting to make eye contact in case it was a nutcase. I was very much alone on a quiet road and at a distinct disadvantage on a bicycle.

The car kept pace with me but stayed just a few inches back. My heart was already pumping from the uphill climb, but it hopped into overdrive. I could almost feel it thumping against my rib cage.

The landscape along the highway on both sides was tall, shrubby and overgrown. A perfect place to ditch a body, I thought darkly.

After all, I'd been concentrating on neighbors and motives and hadn't given any thought to the prospect of a mad killer running loose in town.

I kept my eyes glued ahead of me. The sign welcoming people to Chesterton was still a mere spot in the distance. I pedaled harder. The car pulled up next to me, but I kept my focus on the tiny sign.

"Miss Pinkerton." His voice sounded heavy with dismay, but I was so entirely relieved to hear his familiar tone, I didn't care.

I kept pedaling but slowed to catch my breath. "Detective Briggs, you scared me."

"I apologize." He pulled ahead and stopped the car in the bike path. I had no choice but to stop.

He stepped out of his car and leaned against the back of it, crossing his arms and his ankles. "Just wondering why you happen to be traveling to Chesterton. You didn't mention you had business there when you were in my office."

"Didn't I?"

"No, I think I would have remembered." He tapped the side of his head. "I'm a detective, after all."

"Yes, I can tell by the specially marked license plate on your car. Now, if you don't mind, Detective Briggs, I have some errands to run in Chesterton, and I'd like to be on my way." I stopped and gave him my best wide-eyed blink. "Unless of course there's an ordinance that says a person cannot ride their bike from Port Danby to Chesterton."

He pushed off his car. From my vantage point on my bike seat, he looked extra tall as he looked sternly down at me. "As I said before, Miss Pinkerton, leave the police business to the police."

"Yes, I believe you have said that before. Numerous times."

"That's good. Then I'll leave it at that."

"Wonderful, now if you don't mind, I'll be on my way." I checked the highway for traffic and pedaled around his car. I could feel him watching me for a good fifty yards before I heard his car door slam behind me. The motor started. A few seconds later his car whizzed past, spraying me with grit and dust.

reen Acres Farm Supply was a massive industrial building with pallets of animal feed piled up under a large metal awning. One corner of the large parking lot was dedicated to the storage of heavy equipment like dirt movers and tractors and another was filled with a wall of hay bales. The only vehicle in the lot that was not a truck was Detective Briggs' car . . . and my purple and white bicycle.

I leaned the bike close to the front door, so I could keep an eye on it. The inside of the store was as utilitarian as the outside. Fluorescent bars of light hung from the exposed rafters. The cavernous building was piled high with farm needs like tools, fertilizer and barrels of animal feed. Voices carried in every direction, eventually pinging off the metal walls in tinny echoes. But even with the melee of voices and sounds, I could easily distinguish the deep, measured tone of Detective James Briggs. I tried not to read anything into that.

Briggs was up at the counter that ran the length of the center of the store. Its shelves were filled with bottles and tubes and special tonics and supplements for farm animals. Two cash registers were positioned, one at each end. Briggs was talking to a tall, burly man standing at the far register. The man had on a hat with the store's logo, and he was wearing a pair of crisp denim overalls. Directly across from the counter space, where the two men were talking, were three tall aisles of horse supplies. I skirted around the back of the aisles and came up behind a large barrel filled with stable mucking rakes. I used the rakes like the proverbial potted fern and hid behind them to catch tidbits of the conversation. I wasn't proud of my sneaky efforts, but it was all Briggs' fault. If he wasn't so stubborn, I could have stood in plain view to listen to the chat.

"Beverly Kent?" the man in the hat asked. His big, drum-like voice fit perfectly with his size. "Yesterday? Yeah, she came in. The reason I remember was because she wanted to rent the skid steer. I couldn't understand why she wanted it so early."

"Does she use the skid steer on her farm a lot?" I glimpsed Briggs through the multicolored mucking rakes. He was writing down notes. There was something utterly likable about the fact that he wrote stuff down instead of using a fancy tech device to record things.

"Beverly rents it to scoop up her prize pumpkin for the Port Danby contest. But that's a few weeks off. She was definitely not her usual self. Preoccupied with something. And when I told her the machine had been rented for the week, I about thought she'd break down in tears."

A forklift beeped loudly as it entered the store through the rear opening. I leaned forward to hear over the noise. The rakes parted and I fell through them, creating a nice little clamor of my own.

Both men looked in the direction of the moving muck rakes. My face peered through the forest of handles. Detective Briggs stared at me for a long time before speaking. "I didn't know you owned a horse, Miss Pinkerton."

I pulled myself out and straightened up the display. "Yes, well I don't, but I figured it's never too late to fulfill that dream of a pony on Christmas morning."

"Thank you very much, Mr. Banning. You've been helpful." Detective Briggs put the notepad into his pocket.

"Is Beverly all right? Hope there's nothing wrong," Mr. Banning said.

Detective Briggs looked down for a moment to gather his words. "I'm afraid that Beverly Kent died yesterday."

"Oh, good lord. What a shame. She was such a nice lady. How did she die?"

"That's what we're trying to piece together. Thank you again, Mr. Banning."

"Let me know if there's anything else you need."

"That's appreciated." Detective Briggs walked past me. "You might want to buy that muck rake after all, Miss Pinkerton, because *it's* getting a little thick around here."

CHAPTER 23

I was more than a little miffed at Detective Briggs, but I decided not to let it get in the way of my investigation. And yes, I had decided it was exactly that. There was no harm in me delving a little more into the unseemly death of a Port Danby neighbor. And particularly since circumstances had somehow landed me right in the middle of it.

I waited for Briggs' car to pull out of the farm store parking lot. According to the map on my phone, Featherton's Nursery was just around the corner. Since I was, after all, the owner of a flower shop, I had every right to visit a nursery.

I climbed onto my bicycle and rode down the sidewalk and around the corner. Featherton's Nursery was a quaint wooden cottage with ivory painted siding and gunmetal gray roof tiles. Featherton's Nursery was painted in emerald green letters across a banner that hung along the porch railing. They were having a special sale on ornamental squash plants and rose bushes. There was also a note on the big handwritten sign that this was the last week to order praying mantis eggs for the garden.

Detective Briggs' car was parked out front in one of four parking spots. I pushed my bike past the front steps and stretched up to see what was happening inside. I could see Briggs' blue dress shirt as he browsed a spinning display of seeds. Something told me the man wasn't actually interested in the seeds. Which meant he was probably waiting to speak to the owner.

A sign with a large yellow arrow said *rear garden entrance*. I pushed my bike around the side of the cottage store front and parked it next to a recycling bin. If the detective was waiting inside for the owner, then that meant there was a good chance Mr. Featherton was out back.

I hurried through the gate, hoping I'd get a chance to talk to the owner before Detective Briggs. I needed a tiny bit of revenge on his muck rake comment.

The small cottage in front was a terrific camouflage for the back. Plants, flowers and garden decor stretched on for a good two acres. There was even a long green striped awning set up for shade plants and an entire corner had been turned into a picturesque pond, with a gurgling waterfall and beautiful display of water plants. There were even broad leafed lily pads and bright orange koi swimming beneath them.

I heard someone moving ceramic pots on the back side of the shade garden. I decided I needed to look interested in a purchase. I picked up a five gallon pot containing a tangerine tree and walked to the back of the awning. A man, about fifty, wearing a floppy linen hat and blue knee pads stood up from a line of freshly potted basil plants. He was wearing a t-shirt with the store name. As he turned around, I could see the name Daryl on his nametag. The marigold delivery man had said the owner's name was Daryl Featherton.

As the man walked toward me, I noticed that the thigh of his work pants was stained with some kind of plant residue. Unfortunately, the scent of basil was so strong on his hands, I couldn't smell past it to find out what the stain was from. But it looked a lot like pumpkin or some kind of orange squash.

His fingers and knuckles were stained with soil. He gave them a shake. "How can I help you?" His skin was weathered with deep lines. He had obviously spent a lot of time out in the sun. His gray-blue eyes were set deep in his head, and he had a stiff smile. Or maybe it wasn't a smile at all. He was exactly as one would expect the owner of a nursery to look, with the one exception being a rather large swath of sterile gauze wrapped around his forearm and secured with masking tape. Maybe his first aid kit had run out of medical tape. It definitely looked like a self-made bandage.

"I was just wondering if the fruit on this tree was seedless."

He reached into the base of the plant and pulled out the plastic tab that gave all the pertinent information. Rather rudely, he handed me the tab to read on my own and then headed to the deep sinks set up on the side of the house.

I followed him to the sinks. Naturally. "It says seedless, so I will buy it when I come back with my car. I'm on a bicycle."

He turned the sink on and washed his hands. "That's fine."

"That looks like a pretty bad injury on your arm. Did it happen in the garden or the kitchen? Last year my aunt nearly lost an arm trying to cut open a bagel. Do you know they say half the kitchen related emergency room visits are due to bagels? Who knew a round piece of dough could be so dangerous. I mean there was no mention of donut injuries in the same article." There was a method to my madness. I would fill the air with nonsense and then pop out a few more pertinent questions.

He seemed to be listening to me over the sound of the faucet, but he wasn't responding to anything.

"I own a flower shop in Port Danby. In fact, your truck just delivered the last flats of marigolds to my store. I've heard you are an expert in hybrid seeds."

His face popped my direction. The bagel topic had been a nonstarter, but now I'd grabbed his interest. He turned off the sink. Rather than do the obvious and reach for the paper towel roll hanging above the sink, he shook his hands dry. They were red, raw and chapped, normal for a gardener.

"I could grab you a paper towel," I suggested.

"No thanks." He gave his hands a few more flicks. "How did you hear about the hybrid seeds?" There was just enough suspicion in his tone to give me quick pause on my response. I certainly didn't want to get anyone in trouble. The delivery man seemed to know a bit about it, but if he wasn't supposed to talk about the experimental seeds, then I wasn't going to mention it.

I waved my hand casually. "I'm so new in town, I don't know many names. I've just heard mention of some hybrid pumpkin seeds. Not even sure where I heard it." Maybe Briggs was right in his assessment. I was getting awfully good at lying. Although these white lies had an honorable purpose.

There was just enough of a crease in his already deeply-line forehead to make me worry that I'd brought up the wrong topic. I resorted to humor to break up the awkward moment. "I just thought if you ever come up with long stem roses that last longer than a week, then I'd love to sell them in my shop." I laughed airily, but he didn't even crack a smile.

"I don't sell the hybrid seeds in my shop. I'm working on them for commercial seed and agricultural companies." He was just about to speak again when a woman's voice called out from the side door of the shop. "Daryl, the man is still here. He's waiting to talk to you." The woman who looked about the same age as Daryl but who had taken much more care with her skin, stepped outside for a second. "He says it's important. Some kind of detective."

"I told you I'm coming," Daryl answered angrily. "If you'll excuse me, miss, I'm quite busy. I have a brochure inside that tells you all of the plants we keep in stock and everything we can order. Let's set up a time to talk and see how we can help with your store."

Before he could walk away, I purposely dropped the plastic tab from the citrus tree plant at his feet. "Oops, I better put this back." I leaned down and picked it up, pausing to take a deep whiff of the stain on his pants. With the basil scent washed away, it was easy to smell that the stain on his pants was pumpkin.

"Got it. Thank you. I look forward to talking business with you," I said hastily as he headed into the shop.

The woman exited as he entered. She smiled graciously at me and walked toward the pond area. I wandered behind her, deciding I might gather a little more information. "I'm just going to feed the fish. If you have any questions," she called over her shoulder, "feel free to ask."

"Actually, I just wanted to watch you feed the fish." I stood at the pond's edge and watched as she headed to a small metal bin that was sitting next to an array of fake rocks. She pushed a metal scoop into the bin and pulled out brown pellets.

"Are you Mrs. Featherton?"

She laughed. "No. I just work here. My husband works for the electric company."

"I see."

She sprinkled the pellets along the pond. Gaping mouths with whiskery protrusions popped through the surface. A vibrating collage of sparkling silver and orange fish scales followed as the fish swam over each other to get to the food.

"Wow, they are hungry."

"Yes, and they lack table manners, as you can see." She smiled at me. "I've never seen you before. Are you new to Chesterton?"

"I'm from Port Danby. I just moved there. I'm opening a flower shop."

Her brown eyes rounded. "Oh, you're Miss Pinkerton. I'm Patty. We spoke over the phone about the marigolds. How did those work out for you?"

"They're perfect."

"Great." Her face smoothed to a more somber expression. "I heard that Beverly Kent died yesterday."

"Yes, sadly. So you knew her?"

"Yes. She came into the shop quite often. Although, less frequently lately. I think she and Daryl had a falling out over something. It's a shame to hear she died." Patty dropped the scoop back into the bin. "Well, I better get to watering the roses out back. Let me know if you need anything."

"Thanks. I will."

I headed back toward the shop. Detective Briggs' deep voice drifted through the back screen door, but I couldn't make out the words. The shop interior was small and it would be impossible to hide and listen in on the conversation. It would surely annoy Briggs.

That didn't stop me from walking right inside.

CHAPTER 24

I noticed a discrete, exasperated rise and fall of Detective Briggs' shoulders as I stepped into the shop. He continued with his interview, but I was keenly aware that he was keenly aware that I was listening.

Daryl Featherton was, however, unaffected by my entry into the shop. I browsed the same seed stand I'd seen Briggs looking at when I arrived at the shop. There was no law against it, as far as I knew.

"That's just terrible news," Daryl said sadly. "She'll be missed. I know she was taking medicine for her heart," he continued.

"Yes, well, we haven't narrowed down the cause of death," Briggs said. I held back my smile, thinking how I wasn't the only person spreading boloney. "I found some phone numbers in Mrs. Kent's truck and your store's number was listed. Have you seen Beverly lately?"

It was an easy enough question, but it seemed to throw Daryl off his moment of sorrow. "Here, in the shop? Uh—no." From the corner of my eye, I saw him tap the side of his head. "Wait. Yes she was. She came in here yesterday for a brief stop on her way to the farm store."

I could hear Briggs' pen scratching his notepad. "What was her reason for stopping?"

"Reason for stopping? Oh, yes, she bought a new garden hoe." I could almost hear the tiny sound of a red flag waving over Briggs' head. It was definitely waving over mine. The hoe I had lifted from the garden was new or nicely kept, but it was not brand new. While the handle was pristine, I'd made note of the shovel head as I handed it over. There was enough wearing of the metal to show that it had been used. Possibly even for murder.

"That looks bad," Briggs said.

I peeked over my shoulder to see what he was talking about. He was pointing at the gauze wrapped around Featherton's arm. He had brushed off the question when I brought it up. But then, I had immediately gone off on a wild tangent about bagels, so it wasn't too surprising.

"Oh this. It's nothing. I was sharpening some garden shears and the darn things slipped. Now, if there's nothing else, Detective Briggs, I need to get back to work."

"I almost thought you'd cut yourself carving jack-o'-lanterns," I said abruptly, and instantly had both men's attention. I snuck a secret wink at Briggs as I approached the counter. He looked perturbed. I laughed lightly and pointed to the stain on Featherton's work pants. "I thought since you had pumpkin guts on your pants that you might have been carving those Halloween pumpkins ahead of time."

Briggs took notice of the stain and then waited for Featherton to respond.

The man wiped absently at the stain but didn't say a word.

"It does seem a little early to be carving pumpkins," Detective Briggs said in a way that seemed to require a response.

Mr. Featherton sighed with aggravation. "I'm not carving pumpkins, but just in case there is some law that says I can't carve 'em early —" He marched stridently to a side door that said *Keep Out*.

Briggs glanced my direction, but it was hard to read if he was still annoyed or thankful that I'd pointed out the pumpkin stain. Featherton opened the door to the 'keep out' room and we looked inside. It was a science lab with gram scales and beakers and Bunsen burners. In between the equipment were numerous pumpkins in various degrees of dismemberment. And at the end of the long metal table was a pile of 'pumpkin guts'.

"This is where I work on hybrid seeds." Featherton looked back toward me. "The ones you were asking me about outside."

Briggs slowly turned his face toward me. He was wearing exactly the expression I expected. "Oh, were you now?"

"Yes, Mr. Featherton and I were discussing how his nursery might help my business. Anyhow, it's getting dark and I'm on my bicycle, so good day to both of you."

I made my exit and headed around to the side of the house where I'd parked my bicycle. Patty was pushing some flattened boxes into the recycling bin.

"I suppose you and Mr. Featherton were two of the last people to see Beverly alive," I said casually as I took hold of my bicycle.

She looked up slightly stunned by my statement. "Were we?"

"Mr. Featherton mentioned that Beverly came into the shop yesterday."

With a few good pushes, Patty got the boxes into the bin. "Yes, I guess she was. As a matter of fact, she was walking out as I was walking in. Daryl had the afternoon off, and I came in to run the store for the rest of the day." She seemed to be recalling the previous day. "Sorry, it was rather busy and I was all alone at the counter so the day was a blur. But, yes, Beverly passed me on her way to her truck. She was quite red in the face about something. Why, now that you mention it, she blew right past me without a hello. And that's unusual for her."

"Wow. I guess you had to stay clear of that new garden hoe she was holding, eh?" I laughed to assure her I was joking.

Patty tapped the side of her chin. "Nope. She wasn't holding any garden tools. In fact, she was sort of marching like this." She demonstrated a march while swinging her arms back and forth. "I think I would have remembered if she was holding a long stick in those swinging arms."

"I'm sure of it. Have a good evening." I turned my bike around and rolled it toward the road.

A whistle drew my attention across the parking lot. "Miss Pinkerton, put your bike in the trunk of my car. I'll give you a ride back."

I pushed the bicycle toward him. "That's not necessary."

I reached the car. "That's an order. Not a request. The sun is at a low enough angle that it will be blinding drivers on the highway. It's not a safe time to be riding on the bike path."

"Why, Detective Briggs, it seems you're worried about me. And here I thought I was just a nuisance to you."

"That you are. But I still don't want you out there on that highway." He popped the trunk open, and I pushed the bike to the back. "Besides, I've got some things I want to discuss with you about the case." He lifted the bike into the trunk.

I couldn't hold back my smile.

"Don't get too excited," he warned. "But it seems your intuition and that incredible nose of yours could be of some value in the case. That stain on his pants could have been anything, but you knew it was pumpkin."

I tapped my nose. My smile widened even more.

"I told you not to get too excited."

I sucked my lips in to erase the smile. "Nope. Washing away the excitement. And I've got something to tell you that I think you'll find extremely interesting."

He shut the trunk.

I held up my fingers. "Two questions—do I have to ride in the back?"

"Nope." He opened the passenger door and I sat down. "What's the second question?"

I patted the portable light sitting on the console. "Can we put the siren and light on?"

"Nope." He swung the door shut and climbed into the driver's seat.

Detective Briggs pulled out onto the road. I took the opportunity to glance around his important looking car. Aside from the communication system, there were some other technical looking gadgets.

"Is your weapon in the glove box?" I asked.

"No, it's not. What did you find out that was extremely interesting?"

"There were some inconsistencies in Mr. Featherton's answers." I twisted slightly in my seat. He had one of those perfect profiles, with a strong nose and nicely chiseled jaw line. And eyelashes. Why did men always get the nice eyelashes? It was almost as if mascara companies arranged it in some genetic programming scheme. Give women the skimpy lashes and they will make us all rich.

"Are you referring to the counter height in the lab and position of the pumpkin stain on his pants?" he asked.

I quickly tried to pull the image of the lab up in my head, but I hadn't paid much attention to counter height. "Well, no. What about it?"

"They don't match up. The lab table where he had all the, as you called them, pumpkin guts was much higher than the spot on his pants. Unless, he was holding a pumpkin on his leg as he chopped into it with a knife, the position of the stain doesn't make sense."

"I guess that's why you're the detective, and I'm just a nosy woman with a good nose. I would never have noticed that. But my information was much easier to deduce. Beverly did not come in to buy a garden hoe."

He looked over at me. "No?"

"I spoke to Patty, his assistant. She was out by the recycling bin. She mentioned that Beverly left the nursery yesterday with an angry red face. She didn't even say hello to Patty, and she was marching out of the store with empty hands. I'm pretty sure a garden hoe wouldn't fit in a pocket or purse. And Patty was coming in because Mr. Featherton had the afternoon off."

"Good detective work, Miss Pinkerton." He turned his car onto the highway. He was right. The sun was blindingly low in the sky. I pulled down the visor above my head, and a waterfall of notes and business cards cascaded down from the clip. "Oops." I leaned forward, straining against the seat belt to gather up the pieces.

"That's all right. Just leave it."

The last piece of paper I picked up was a piece of notepaper with the name Rachel and a phone number. Suddenly, I was trying to picture Rachel, no doubt, with her long blonde hair, baby blue eyes and . . .

"Miss Pinkerton?"

I turned to look at him.

"Did you hear me?"

"I'm sorry. I was temporarily distracted."

"Even though Featherton's stories don't line up with the truth, what motive would he have to kill Beverly Kent? After you left, I asked a few questions about how they knew each other and it seemed to be strictly a customer and merchant relationship."

I sat back to give it some thought. "It's true there is no motive that jumps out of all this." And then my mind went to the seeds. "Except there is one thing that keeps crackling in my head. Hybrid seeds."

"How could his scientific hobby give him motive for murder?"

"I'm not sure, but I know Beverly's neighbor, Virginia, used his special hybrid pumpkin seeds in her patch."

We turned onto Culpepper Road. Both of us instinctively looked down Dawson Grove. It was quiet. Virginia's house had a light on, but her neighbor's empty house was dark.

"You live on Loveland Terrace, right?"

"Yes. Thank you."

"How do you know what kind of seeds Virginia used?"

"It's just circumstantial, but I found an empty packet of Featherton's hybrid pumpkin seeds in her service porch when I was—"

"Searching for your lost key?" He finished with a throat clearing. "I'll make note of the pumpkin seeds."

We drove along Myrtle Place. Hawksworth Manor loomed high above the other houses. An involuntary shiver raced through me when I thought about being locked in the dark entryway.

Detective Briggs missed very little. "Are you cold?"

"Yes, a bit. I think I'll take a hot bath when I get home. Thank you again for the ride. It's this first house."

He pulled into the driveway. We climbed out. As Briggs was

pulling my bike from the trunk, Dash pulled into his driveway in his truck.

Dash climbed out. His smile faded when he saw Detective Briggs. Briggs was wearing a mask of stone as well. Dash didn't stay to talk or even say hello. He disappeared quickly into his house.

I took hold of my bike. "Thanks again for the ride."

Briggs pulled out of the chilly trance he'd been in and looked at me. "No problem. I'll see you later." He climbed back inside the car.

I pushed my bike up to the porch and watched as he drove off.

After the glacial moment between Detective Briggs and Dash, I was really going to need that hot bath.

CHAPTER 25

I'd set up a convenient potting station on the back wall, and my forethought and planning had paid off. I was able to quickly plant all the marigolds in the small pots with the shop name. I stood back and admired them. They would be a fun marketing tool for the shop's opening.

I walked over to the basin sink and washed my hands. As the dirt ran down the drain, I thought about the day before at the nursery. While there was no way to come to a concise motive, there sure were a lot of inconsistencies in Mr. Featherton's answers. And if Beverly hadn't gone to the nursery to buy anything, why was she there? And why on earth would Featherton lie about it? There were so many unanswered questions and fuzzy details it made my head spin. When I got home tonight, I planned to make a list of the things we'd learned since the discovery of Beverly's body.

I turned off the faucets and reached for a paper towel but then stopped and shook them, using Featherton's technique. But I grew impatient fast and grabbed a towel. It was a strange habit for a man who had to spend a lot of time washing his hands.

My phone rang as I tossed the used towel in the waste basket. I picked it up. "Hey, Mom."

"Hello, my sweet, how is everything going?"

"Very well, thanks. How's Dad?"

"He's walking around like he's wearing shoes filled with helium. He's been chosen to be a judge in a craft beer contest."

I laughed. "That sounds right up his alley." She continued on about some of the details, but my mind drifted to the notion that there must be judges for the pumpkin contest. I was still convinced Beverly's death had something to do with the contest. I made a mental note to find out about the judges and pushed my focus back to the phone call. Mom was still talking, so she hadn't noticed my momentary lack of attention. Hopefully she hadn't mentioned anything too pertinent like the hiding place for the family will while I drifted off.

"By the way, Lacey, thought you might be interested. Jacob has been promoted to CEO of the perfumery. Apparently, his father decided to retire."

"That's nice." I hoped that she would eventually stop obsessing about the fact that her only daughter gave up a life of luxury and, no doubt, perpetual heartbreak to live a quaint, idyllic life by the sea.

"Are you and Dad ready for that cruise next month?" I had given them a two week cruise around Europe for their thirtieth wedding anniversary. I thought it was the coolest gift ever. When I gave it to them, I'd expected them to dance around the room like I used to do as a kid on Christmas morning. But they were both a little perplexed and even dismayed. Almost as if they thought I was sending them off to a work camp or retirement home. After I sent them a lot of pictures of other people their age sipping wine and chatting as they watched Bavarian castles float past on the shore, they started to warm up to the idea.

"Ugh," Mom grunted. "I don't know if I'll ever be ready. You need a lot of fancy clothes for those cruises. Then there are the warm clothes for the excursions on shore. But I'll manage. Your dad insists the clothes in his closet are fine. So I will either have to sit at a different dining table and pretend we're not together or we'll order room service so we don't have to leave the cabin."

"That's silly. Remind Dad if he's going to judge the craft beer contest he'll need a nice modern suit. Then he'll have one for the cruise."

"And that's why you're my brilliant little girl."

The goat bell clanged, and Elsie walked in with a plate of cookies. "Well, Mom, Elsie just walked in with—" I took a whiff. "Freshly baked snickerdoodles, so I've got to go."

"All right, sweetie. Talk soon. Bye."

Elsie was admiring my flower pots as I hung up. I went straight to the cookies. Nevermore, who had tagged along for the day, circled my legs hoping they were for him. The cat taking action for a cookie immediately sent Kingston into dance mode. "Neither of you are getting a cookie. They're for me."

Elsie took a moment to scratch Nevermore behind the ears and then straightened. "Do you think I could have a few of these pots? I just need three. I think they'll be a nice addition to my seating area."

Lester's tables had filled up faster than Elsie's this morning. She'd spent a good hour dragging around her tables and chairs, looking for a more suitable arrangement. Soon there wouldn't be any cement left on the walkway in front of her bakery.

"I have quite a few. You can have three. It'll be good advertisement too." Elsie walked to the potter's table and surveyed the choices before picking up the pots with the biggest blooms.

"Hold on." I walked to the center island and opened the drawer with the museum wax. I pulled a chunk of wax from the jar and put it in an empty pot. "I use this to keep the vases from falling off the shelves. Stick a wad under each pot and then stick them to the table. Otherwise, one good breeze and the flowers will be gone."

"Thanks, Pink. You're a doll. Enjoy the cookies."

"That will not be a problem," I said over a mouthful of buttery cinnamon cookie.

Elsie walked out and Lola popped in right after, not even giving the goat bell a chance to stop clanging from Elsie's exit.

"I need your help, Pink." Lola made a bee line for the cookie plate.

"What do you need?"

"I'm trying to hang up a Halloween garland across my front

window. I need you to hold up one end. I've got extra too, if you want to hang one across your window."

"Sounds like a deal. Let me just pour Nevermore some food before he trips me on my face." I filled the cat's food bowl and dropped some sunflower seeds and cat food into Kingston's bowl.

We walked across to Lola's shop. She had a small, primitive step ladder, a relic I'd seen in the store, set up in front of the window. Lola picked up the garland, a glittery strand of pumpkins, ghosts and bats and carried it to the step ladder.

"Will that hold you?" I asked. "The rungs look kind of brittle."

"Of course. If you know anything about antiques, you know that the old stuff was made way better than the new."

"Good point." I picked up my end of the garland and held it as she draped and taped the garland festively across the front window. I could see Elsie in the reflection, sticking the marigold pots to the tables. They looked cute.

Lola moved the ladder and took the last end from my hand. Something in the distance caught her eye. "Ooh, I like the view from up here," she said excitedly enough that the ladder wobbled beneath her.

I grabbed hold of the sides to steady it. "Watch yourself up there. Sturdy ladder or not, your bones will break if they hit that cement."

She pulled her attention from whatever had caught it and finished taping up the garland. "How does it look?"

I backed up and stared up at the newly decorated window. "Very Halloweenish."

Lola climbed down from the ladder and motioned with her head. "If you're wondering why the view was so nice, check out the tall stack of gorgeous coming down the sidewalk."

I followed the direction of her head motioning. Dash was walking along my side of the sidewalk with Captain trotting along next to him. "Oh, it's Dash."

"Do you know him?"

"He lives next door."

"That's right. I forgot you moved into the Beeker's old place. Lucky girl. I sure would love to watch that man mow his lawn." She elbowed me. "If you know what I mean."

"I assume you mean you want to watch him mow his grass. He is very nice though."

Lola rolled her eyes. "Please, very nice. A stroll through a park is very nice. Watching a good movie while chewing on Milk Duds is very nice. Living next door to the brilliantly beautiful Dashwood Vanhouten, the third is spectacularly nice. Look, he's nearing Mod Frock. Cue Kate Yardley *now*."

And as if Lola had some uncanny ability to predict the future, Kate Yardley, the owner of the vintage clothing boutique two shops down, stepped out onto the sidewalk. Dash's reaction to seeing her was less than enthusiastic. Kate Yardley, who I had only exchanged a few good mornings with, was a beautiful, curvy thirty something who changed her hair color dramatically from week to week. Right now it was a pale, Marilyn Monroe style blonde. She'd tied a thick paisley scarf around it like a hair band. She was wearing a tight fitting mod style dress and short black boots. I had to admit I was envious of her fashion sense. She could pull together a great look and all with clothes from a different decade. I had yet to walk into her store, but I was sure it would be a fun place to shop. One thing I'd noted about Kate was that she wasn't nearly as friendly as the other shopkeepers on the street. That might have been why I hadn't ventured into her store yet.

But she was certainly friendly with Dash. She must have touched him five times in the first few moments of their meeting, a meeting that seemed purely accidental to him but seemed quite planned on her part.

Lola stood next to me and watched the scene down the street unfold. "Supposedly, they were a thing a few years back. Kate insists she broke his heart. But every time I see her shoot out of her store like a hungry bear when that six foot plus pot of honey walks by, I wonder if it wasn't the other way around."

"There does seem to be a lopsided amount of energy in the greeting. There's Lester at my door with a cup of hot coffee. Something tells me he's come for a few of my flowers. I'm thinking of finally taking a look around Kate's shop later. She's had a shiny pair of boots in her window the last few days that keep calling my name as I ride past. And I think it would be neighborly of me to finally introduce myself."

"I'll go. I could use some new earrings. Just stop by when you're ready."

CHAPTER 26

I had finished ordering the last of the fresh flowers, greenery and baby's breath for opening day. It would arrive two days ahead to give me plenty of time to put together pretty arrangements. Nevermore had curled up beneath the potter's table, and Kingston slept quietly with his beak tucked under his wing. I decided to see if Lola was ready to walk down to the Mod Frock. I wanted give those boots a closer look.

I was surprised to see Detective Briggs' car pull up in front of the shop. He didn't get out but slid down his passenger side window. "Miss Pinkerton, the shop looks nice."

I leaned down to the open window. "Thank you. I'm quite thrilled with the way it turned out."

"Just thought you'd want to know. The lab results showed that the blood on the hoe did not belong to Beverly Kent."

"Huh, that's interesting. Maybe it was a rat or pumpkin eating pest like you first thought."

"No, they said it was definitely human blood. I'm heading out to the Kent house right now to have another look at things."

I bit my lip, thinking how much I would love to do the same. He seemed to read my mind.

"I'll let you know if I find anything. You get on with your day."

"Yes, I know. Official police business and all that. Well then, like you said, I'll get on with my day."

"See you later, Miss Pinkerton."

Lola came out of her shop with her purse. She watched Detective Briggs turn the corner as she headed across the street. "You have Dash as a neighbor and the illustrious Detective Briggs, who is as rare to spot as a striped cheetah, makes a stop on the street just to chat with you. I'm proud to call you my friend, Pink."

"Yes, it's a glamorous life I lead." I punctuated my words with an eye roll. "Shall we?"

"Yes."

We strolled past Elsie's tables. Two of them were filled. Maybe the flower idea had worked. Lester hadn't put out the flowers he'd traded his special hazelnut brew for, but I was sure he would soon enough.

The Mod Frock Vintage Clothing boutique was as vibrant and lofty as its owner. The nearly blinding white lacquer paint on the exterior was thankfully punctuated with arched glass windows. The wall of bright white, a white that put to shame a hill of freshly fallen snow, was bordered by a slim entryway lined with used brick and an ivory door with a peep window that mirrored the arches of the front windows. Miss Yardley had purchased thick doormats emblazoned with the Mod Frock logo. I decided that since she'd 'lifted' my sidewalk chalkboard display idea, I could 'lift' her logo doormat idea.

"I noticed that after you started posting chalk signs about your grand opening, Kate suddenly had a chalkboard display too," Lola muttered as we walked inside.

"Yes, I noticed that."

I stood inside, mouth gaping. As proud as I'd been of the way my shop looked, I was feeling a bit deflated. My eyes swept around the store. There was no denying Kate Yardley's wonderful sense of style and taste. Upon entering, a customer's eyes were pulled in every direction. The south wall contained four impressive sets of mounted elk antlers displaying colorful scarves, long strands of beads and silver hoop earrings. The shabby chic milk paint tables in the center of the store were cluttered with mod Twiggy inspired confections like pill box hats, neon plastic bauble bracelets and union jack t-shirts. The racks were filled to the brim with the colors, fabrics and styles of yesteryear, a time when wild paisleys, dangerously short minis and glossy knee high boots ran wild in the streets. Thank goodness we figured out it was a style that should never be covered by layers of time.

Kate came out of the back and gave me a quick once over. "I have the perfect dress for you. Size 8?"

"Size 6," I corrected.

She stopped to do a double take. "Maybe you're retaining water," she said casually.

I shot a *look* at Lola, who winked back at me in return.

"Actually, I wanted to formally introduce myself." I followed Kate to the rack where she was rummaging through some dresses.

Kate looked up at me. She had flawless skin and was even prettier up close. She removed her hands from the dresses for a second to shake mine. "Kate and you're Lacey. Or Pink, according to Elsie. Nice to meet you. Now where did that dress go to? It has a long zipper up the front and—"

"I was interested in the shiny black boots in the window. What size are they?"

She stopped looking for the dress and turned back to me. "Those boots are gone. Theresa Jones was in here just yesterday afternoon. She bought them. Although they were a little snug around her thick calves. I guess she's feeling a little renewed now that—" She stopped and seemed to think better of churning out gossip with the tragedy still so fresh. "I joked with her, telling her she had to stop looking so happy or people would think she killed Bev herself."

Or maybe not.

Lola and I both gasped simultaneously. (*And silently.*) It seemed Kate was the type to say whatever was on her mind.

"You didn't." Lola was the first to find her tongue. "How on earth did she react to that?"

"She was so angry and upset I thought she'd throw the boots back in my face. Guess I wasn't expecting such a strong reaction." Kate shrugged, vibrating the long strands of beads she had hanging around her neck. "But she took the boots anyhow. I can let you know the second I get in another pair."

"That would be great." Suddenly, I had an urge to get out to Beverly's house and see just what Detective Briggs was finding during his inspection. It seemed as if the list of possible suspects just kept growing.

CHAPTER 27

*D*etective Briggs' car was still parked out front of the Kent farm. He wasn't standing in the pumpkin patch. I walked into the yard just as he was coming around from the back of the house. He didn't look all that surprised to see me, and he didn't look as annoyed as usual. I took both as a good sign that he'd take me along on his inspection of the property.

"I wondered what took you so long," Briggs commented as he walked around to the front porch.

"I went shopping. And to be honest, I wasn't too sure how I would be received." I followed along next to him. "But now that I know you were expecting me, is there something specific we're looking for?"

He reached up and ran his fingers along the top of the door jamb. "I was hoping to find a key. The back door was locked, and I couldn't find an open window."

"So we're breaking and entering?"

Briggs stopped and looked at me with a minor twisted grin. "You are. I'm a detective."

"In that case—" I walked over to the large potted rubber plant at the corner of the porch. I reached inside the plant and circled the base of it until my fingertips hit metal. I pulled the key out. "I'll just use a key rather than get arrested."

"The potted plant," he mused. "Can't believe I didn't think of that."

"It's kind of an obvious place to hide a key. Which also makes it an unsafe place to hide a key." I turned the lock and smiled at him. "Maybe your detective brain pushed it off as too simple."

"Yes, I'm sure that's it." He put his hand up. "Uh, I'll go in first." He patted his shirt pocket. "Badge, remember?"

I waved my hand with a flourish. "Of course, after you."

The house had been closed up for two days, and it smelled like two day old fried chicken. "You haven't been in the house yet?" I asked.

"Actually, I sent Chinmoor in the first evening to look around. He must have been the one to lock the back door. He found no evidence of foul play and everything looked as expected. At that time, there wasn't much to go on. But I thought we might find some evidence that could help figure out what happened to Beverly. Just not sure what we're looking for yet."

I had a wide grin by the time he was done. "And why do you look like the Cheshire cat right now, Miss Pinkerton?"

"No reason except you said *we* twice in your last statement."

"Did I? I was talking about Chinmoor and me."

"Oh, right, your partner."

"He's not my partner." He headed toward the kitchen.

I decided to stray into the first bedroom. There was a sweater on the bed and a brush and comb on the dresser. It seemed this was the bedroom Beverly used. A touch of sadness swept over me as I looked around at her things, her bedroom slippers, hand lotion, reading glasses on the nightstand, all waiting for her to come in for the evening.

A white antique vanity and stool were in the corner near the window. A velvet lined jewelry box, the vintage kind with the tiny ballerina that starts twirling to music, sat open on the vanity. The ballerina stood perfectly still, and there was no music. Three necklaces were piled carelessly next to the box. A few bracelets and rings still sat inside.

I thought back to Beverly as she lay in her pumpkin patch. I couldn't remember seeing any jewelry. Since I'd touched her neck to check for signs of a pulse, I was sure there was no necklace. Maybe she had taken them off to work outside. That certainly made sense. What didn't make sense was why she would've opened the jewelry box and dumped the necklaces into a heap next to it. And why would she have been wearing three necklaces at once?

I got up and circled the room. Things certainly looked in order and as if Beverly's day had started in the normal way. Her slippers were tucked neatly next to the bed, and her bath robe was hanging from a hook on the door. Other than the jewelry, everything was neat and orderly. It seemed Beverly was a fastidious housekeeper.

I walked to the nightstand and picked up the magazine she'd been reading called Farmhouse Basics. It had articles about raising chickens, canning preserves and baking the perfect biscuit. Everything you would expect in a magazine called Farmhouse Basics. As I returned the magazine to its place on the nightstand, I noticed an article that had been torn out from a newspaper. I picked it up.

"Local Nursery hits the big time. Daryl Featherton's hybrid seeds are about to find a home with Buffy Seed company, one of the biggest seed distributors in the country. Featherton has been perfecting a pumpkin seed that grows what he claims are the biggest, hardiest squash in the world. The contract has not been signed yet, but prospects look good for the Chesterton business owner."

"Miss Pinkerton," Detective Briggs poked his head into the room. "You haven't touched anything, have you?"

"Only this. I found it under a magazine. Oh, and I touched the magazine. But that's it." I handed it to him and let him read it as I did one last sweep of the room with my eyes. A glint of silver underneath the vanity caught my attention. I walked over and reached down for the piece of foil. It was the inside of a gum wrapper.

I lifted it to my nose. "Spearmint."

"What?"

I turned back to him and held up the wrapper. "Spearmint gum."

"Maybe Beverly liked chewing gum," he suggested as he tucked the article into his pocket. "Interesting article. Not sure how it would connect Featherton to a motive. Unless we can find something that actually puts him here at the farm, it'll be hard to find a reason to bring him in for questioning."

"True." I held up the gum wrapper. "But this might be evidence that puts someone else at the scene. Someone who has a motive. The old standby—jealousy."

"Oh?"

"Theresa Jones is married to William Jones."

"The fisherman?"

"Yes, and back in high school, he and Beverly were sweethearts. According to Lola, from Lola's Antiques, William and Beverly were still overly fond of each other." I stopped and a spark of light came to me. "The jewelry box. I wonder if it has anything to do with the class ring that William bought back from Lola."

"Miss Pinkerton, you've lost me. What about the gum wrapper?"

"Theresa Jones chews gum. When I met her she had a big wad in her mouth. She was working that thing like a pro. I smelled spearmint on her breath. She might even chew it just to smell something fresher than dead fish all day." I lifted the wrapper again. "This was a stick of spearmint gum. It was under the vanity where, oddly enough, Beverly's jewelry box was open. For some reason, she left her necklaces in a pile on the vanity."

"So someone might have been looking for something in the jewelry box? You think the motive was to steal? The rest of the house seems untouched."

"Not stealing for money. Earlier this week there was an incident with William's old class ring. Theresa had sold it to Lola with a box of old things she was getting rid of. William came into the shop frantically looking for the ring. According to Lola, it was strung on a thin gold chain. William bought it back from Lola."

"You think he bought it to give it back to Beverly?"

"If they had been high school sweethearts—"

"She probably wore that necklace when they were a couple," he finished for me.

"It seems we make a good team, Detective Briggs."

He responded with a very guarded smile.

CHAPTER 28

I finished drying the two dishes I'd used for my grilled cheese dinner and followed the moonlight out to my front porch. Kingston had long since gone to sleep, but evening hours were Nevermore's time to shine. The cat, tail straight in air, padded down the front steps to chase moths and other night creatures.

I pulled out my notepad. I'd decided to write down all the possible clues in Beverly's death and see if I could make sense of any of them. I sat down on the top step and was just about to start when I noticed Nevermore's tail fluff out in full defense mode. I looked in the direction the cat was staring.

Dash was coming across his driveway with Captain at his side. Nevermore stood stiff as a statue, apparently thinking no one could see him if he didn't move, even standing beneath the glow of the streetlights. When he saw that Captain was one of those dogs that had zero interest in cats he returned to his moth hunt.

Dash was wearing a blue flannel shirt that went nicely with his suntanned skin. He had splashed on some aftershave. It took me a second to block it out so as not to be overwhelmed by the spicy scent of it.

"Mind if I join you?" he asked. I briefly wondered what woman in her right mind would say no to that.

"Not at all." I scooted over.

Captain plopped down at the bottom of the steps, and Dash sat next to me.

"Working on a business plan?" he asked.

"Now what kind of business woman would I be if I started the plan just a few days from actually opening the business?"

"Very good point, and it shows just how much I know about business." He leaned back on his hands and stretched out his long legs. His ankles ended up three steps down. Sitting next to him really put his size into perspective. "I spent the day working on a big, rusty fishing trawler that is so old she needs to be put out of her misery. It was a long day."

"I'm sorry to hear that." As much as I enjoyed a visit from my neighbor, I was also anxious to get to my list. I decided to write down a few things while he seemed occupied with the night sky.

My pen scratched out some bubbles. I put initials under each bubble for the three people who I had narrowed down on my suspect list, namely Theresa Jones, Virgina Hopkins and Daryl Featherton. I quickly wrote class ring, jealousy, chewing gum and cheery mood in the bubble over T.J. The bubble for V.H. had pumpkin in shears and pumpkin competition. And the D.F. bubble was even less inspired with hybrid pumpkin seeds and argument with Beverly.

"It's a good thing that isn't a business plan, otherwise I'd advise you to shutter the doors before you even open."

Astonishingly, I'd nearly forgotten about Dash sitting next to me.

"I suppose it does look a little crazy."

He sat forward and pointed to the pumpkin competition. "That comical pumpkin contest is such a big deal. Now it won't be much of a competition without Beverly. Don't know what our even more comical mayor will do. He takes his judge position very seriously, but there is hardly a need for him at all."

I looked over at Dash. "Mayor Price is the judge?"

He laughed. "Most important part of his silly job. Also Helen Voight, in the yellow house at the end of our street, is the co-judge. If there's such a thing. So have you been up to Hawksworth Manor at night? We could go. There are always plenty of unexplained sounds to curdle the blood and set a vivid imagination on fire."

I shook my head. "No thanks. It wasn't a lot of fun during the day. It sounds even less inviting at night."

He laughed. "Thought you were more adventurous than that."

"I am. But only when there's a lot of light."

"Do you always hang out with detectives?" The question came so unexpectedly and out of thin air that I was almost not sure I'd heard it.

"If you're talking about Detective Briggs, then we weren't *hanging* out. He was giving me a ride home because I'd stayed out too late to ride safely home on my bicycle. He was just watching out for one of Port Danby's citizens."

"Hey, Lacey, I meant nothing by it. Sorry for bringing it up." He'd obviously detected the bit of anger in my tone.

I had to admit the icy exchange of glances the night before, when Briggs dropped me at home, still had me curious. Since he'd brought the subject up first, I decided I had every right to pry a bit. "Do you and the detective know each other well?"

He paused. "Not really. We grew up in the same schools in Chesterton, and we were on the high school football team together. But that's where the acquaintance ends."

"I see. Just curious." Growing up with someone and playing on the same football team seemed like it needed a better word than acquaintance, but maybe they hardly ever spoke during those years.

I yawned and stretched. "Seems the long day is finally getting to me. I think I'll head inside."

"Yep, I'm pretty tired myself." He stood up and politely offered me his hand. I put mine in his. It was a strong hand, and the callus of hard work was built up on the palm and fingertips. He popped me to my feet and bowed his head. "Good night, neighbor." He walked down the steps and stopped at the bottom. "Try not to get locked in any haunted houses tomorrow."

I smiled. "I'll try my best to avoid that."

CHAPTER 29

*L*ola opened the front door to the shop as I finished filling a nifty little triple tiered display with note cards. I looked toward the front window. A clammy mist had covered the town for most of the morning, but the sun was finally starting to make some headway.

"It's starting to clear up," I said. "Not that it matters now. The bike ride to the shop already sent my freshly washed hair into curlicue overdrive." I pulled on one strand. It bounced back like a coiled spring. "My hair is going to be the one drawback of living by the sea."

Lola palmed her curly red hair as it stuck out from under a khaki colored fedora. "And now you see why I don't even bother with a flat iron. Waste of time, energy and money." She patted the top of her fedora. "Hats are a much cheaper way to go, and they don't give you split ends."

I laughed. "I'll have to remember that."

Lola walked over and lightly rubbed Kingston's shiny black head. He had gotten used to her much faster than most people.

"I think my bird might have a crush on you." I finished flattening the card shipping boxes.

"At least someone does. That dating site thing has been a bust so far. Only a bunch of goobers on there. The one good prospect has already been snapped up by someone else it seems because he disappeared off the site."

"Don't be too discouraged, Lola. You'll find someone when the time is right."

"Says the woman who has the eye of Detective James Briggs and who lives right next door to Dashwood Vanhouten." She pressed her arm against her stomach. "Anyhow, I didn't come in here to remind myself how pathetic my social life is. I've got a terrible craving for one of Franki's cheese omelets. Are you game for a trip to the diner?"

"I could eat. I only had time for a banana this morning. My alarm went off, and I hit snooze a dozen times before the clock just shut down itself. I guess it was tired of getting slammed on the head. I'm done with the display so we can go now."

"Great."

We headed out, and I locked up behind me. We walked past the Coffee Hutch. Lester had added a potted marigold to each table just like Elsie. I wondered what would happen next? Cushions on the chairs? We continued on to the diner.

"Where did you go yesterday after our trip to the Mod Frock? I knocked on the flower shop door about an hour after we got back, and you were already gone."

While Lola had slowly become the friend I could tell stuff, even secret stuff to, I hadn't mentioned anything about the murder investigation to her. I was sure Detective Briggs did not want me broadcasting clues and theories all over a town that thrived on gossip.

"I felt like taking a bike ride along the beach."

"You've got way more energy than me, my friend. The shop was slow in the afternoon, so I stretched out on that old, Victorian fainting couch and had myself a nice nap."

"Huh, I guess it's convenient to have furniture like fainting couches right in the middle of the sales floor. And if it's any consolation, I fell asleep by eight last night, and, as I mentioned, I was still fighting the alarm this morning."

We walked into the diner and were instantly greeted with the smell of bacon and waffles. The mixture of scents drifting out through the cook's window nearly made me dizzy. I was far more hungry than I'd realized.

Franki waved from behind the coffee station. "Take a seat anywhere, girls. And grab a few menus on the way."

Franki walked over to take our order. She plunked down a bottle of ketchup. "New batch I just made this morning."

I was confused. "You make your own ketchup?"

Both Franki and Lola looked almost insulted that I didn't know. "Franki's ketchup is world renowned." Lola twisted her lips in thought. "Wait, what does that mean? Anyhow, her ketchup is famous here in Port Danby. And it just so happens I'm going to need it because I'm having a cheese omelet."

"I'll have scrambled eggs and a biscuit." I handed Franki our menus, and she walked away.

Lola watched that Franki was out of earshot and leaned forward to talk, just in case earshot was farther than she thought. "Although if you ask me, sometimes Franki puts in just a bit too much nutmeg. Makes me think I'm eating pumpkin pie instead of meatloaf."

"I'll bet." I relaxed back for a second and then popped forward again. "Did you say pumpkin pie?" I grabbed the ketchup and untwisted the cap before Lola could utter yes.

I took a whiff. "Woo hoo, you are right. There's nutmeg in that ketchup. Interesting," I muttered to myself, but Lola figured I was talking to her. My mind shot straight back to the ketchup stain on Beverly's blouse. I wondered if she had eaten in the diner the morning of her death. Or maybe she had a bottle of ketchup at home.

"Why is it interesting? I think a lot of people put spices in their homemade condiments."

"Yes, I'm sure they do. Does Franki ever sell her ketchup?"

"Gosh, someone was impressed with the smell. You haven't even tasted it yet. Maybe you won't like it."

"I won't. I'm not a big ketchup eater." I skirted around for a good response. "I just thought it would be extra income for her, you know, with all those hungry teens to feed."

"Huh, good point. But she doesn't sell any. She has a hard enough time keeping it stocked in her diner."

Franki was returning with two glasses of ice water. I knew Lola was going to ask me a dozen follow up questions, but I just couldn't let the opportunity pass. That ketchup stain had been just that, a stain. But what if there had been more to it than Beverly accidentally swiping her shirt with a ketchup covered finger.

I debated letting it go, but the question rolled off my tongue before I could stop it. "Franki, was Beverly Kent in the diner the morning of her death?"

I could feel Lola's wide-eyed gaze on me as I waited for Franki's response. "Beverly, not sure. Why?"

"It could be something Detective Briggs will want to know."

"I knew it," Lola said. "I knew you were up to something with him."

"I'm not, Lola. But you seem to forget, I was accidently thrust into her death by finding her in the pumpkin patch."

Franki shook her head. "Come to think of it, I hadn't seen Beverly in the diner in at least a week. I think she was trying one of those carbohydrate free diets. Her doctor suggested she lose some weight." Franki sighed sadly. "Guess that's not going to help her now."

"Thanks, Franki. I'll let Detective Briggs know."

"I'll bet," Lola muttered with her mouth on her straw.

Franki tilted her head in question. "Does he think Beverly was murdered?"

I knew I'd be opening a big can of worms, but I was sure I now had some important evidence for Detective Briggs. "I'm not really at liberty to say. I think the detective is just looking at all angles."

Fortunately, a customer across the aisle called Franki away. That still left my highly curious friend sitting at the same table. And she wasn't leaving, so I was going to have to answer some questions.

I leaned forward. "I can't say any more about it." I dropped my voice to a whisper. "Beverly did not die from a heart attack. There is some evidence of foul play." Her mouth formed an O, but I stopped her from blurting anything out. "But don't say a word to anyone or

Detective Briggs will put me on my bicycle and roll me straight out of town. Promise?"

"Yes, of course. Wow. Poor Beverly." She fingered the ketchup bottle. "But what does it have to do with Beverly coming into the diner."

"It doesn't. I'm not sure if it means anything. I'm just looking for evidence."

"Ooh, like a real private investigator."

I pushed down a smile. "I do like a good mystery. Which reminds me, on the morning before Beverly's mur—death, we ate at the diner. Virginia Hopkins was here too. I remember because she was angrily sawing at her steak."

"That's right. I remember."

"Did you happen to notice if she was eating ketchup on that steak?"

Lola sat back with a satisfied grin. "That I can answer easily. No. Virginia gets hives from tomatoes. I know that because once, when I was with my parents eating dinner here, Virginia ate a piece of Franki's meatloaf. She didn't realize the ketchup was mixed into the meat. She swelled up like a pink balloon. The ambulance had to take her to the hospital. Scared me off of ketchup and tomatoes for months."

"Then that's a definitive *no* on Virginia and ketchup."

"Yep. Hey, did I just give you some evidence? Maybe I should take up investigative work." She sat back with a laugh. "Nah, sounds as boring as watching the dust settle on a coffee table."

Sometimes it was as if we were polar opposites.

CHAPTER 30

*A*fter our late breakfast revealed a plethora of interesting goodies, I made the excuse to Lola that I needed a walk before heading back to the shop. Lola wasn't big on walks or bike rides or exercise in general, so I knew she would head back to her store, leaving me on my own to slip into the police station.

I didn't want Lola to see me cross to the station, so I continued along Harbor Lane and turned down Pickford Way, deciding I could catch a few moments on the beach before making my way back to the station. My detour to throw my friend off the scent landed me right in front of the wharf, where conveniently enough, Detective Briggs had just parked his car. He hadn't seen me walk up as he stepped out of his car.

"Good day to you, sir," I said cheerily.

He spun around. I wondered what kind of expression I'd be met with this time. His eyes were covered by dark sunglasses, but I was pleased to see his half smile beneath the shades. "Miss Pinkerton, it seems wherever I find myself, you are nearby."

I stopped in front of him. "Don't let it go to your head. It's a small town, after all."

He nodded. "True enough. I won't let it go to my head."

"Where are you going?" I asked sticking by his side as he headed toward the marina.

"Police business. Where are you headed?"

"Pseudo police business."

"I don't believe there is such a thing as pseudo police business."

A group of seagulls had gathered in front of us to eat up some spilled potato chips, I used that as my opportunity to stop him. "I have some information I think you'll be interested in." I could see my reflection in his glasses and the marina behind me. Theresa was busy moving fish from a basket to a wheel barrow. She had a mouthful of chewing gum.

"Lola and I were at the diner, and I discovered that Franki makes her own ketchup."

"That's hardly headline news, Miss Pinkerton. I've eaten her home-made ketchup many times."

"I'm getting to the headline part. Remember when I said that the ketchup stain on Beverly's shirt reminded me of pumpkin pie? Well, it wasn't pumpkin pie. It was nutmeg. One of Franki's ingredients. The ketchup must have been Franki's because you don't find nutmeg in commercial ketchup."

"Maybe Beverly had something to eat at the diner."

I enthusiastically patted his chest. An awkward moment of silence followed. "Oops, sorry. I didn't mean to touch your—" I circled my hand in front of him. "Your officialness. Anyhow, I asked Franki if Beverly had eaten at the diner that day. She had not. In fact, Beverly was on a diet and hadn't eaten at the diner for at least a week."

I could see the gears turning in his mind even with his nice, dark eyes covered in sunglasses. "Then how could she have gotten the ketchup on her blouse? Maybe Franki sold her a bottle."

"Lola said Franki has enough trouble keeping the diner stocked with it, but you could always check Beverly's kitchen just to be sure."

The two little lines creased the side of his mouth. His crooked smile seemed to be a mix of amusement and irritation. "If I didn't know any better, Miss Pinkerton, I'd say you were trying to tell me how to do my job."

"No, never. I can see that you are quite able to do it without my guidance." The seagulls parted and he walked on.

Naturally, I scooted along next to him. "Are you on your way to talk to Theresa?"

"As a matter of fact I am."

Theresa had left the fish cleaning station and climbed back onto the deck of the fishing boat. She was talking to William. Both of them looked quickly back at us.

"I think they know you're coming to see them."

"Seems that way," he said calmly.

"Is it because of the gum wrapper?"

"A gum wrapper isn't quite enough evidence to question someone." He stopped before we reached the boat. "Franki's son Taylor works out at Virginia's farm after school. He mentioned to Officer Chinmoor that he'd seen Theresa go into Beverly's house two days ago. He thought it wasn't right that she was looking around the house, so he decided to tell the police."

"Ah, then the gum wrapper was a good piece of evidence?"

"It was." He couldn't hold back his smile any longer. "Good work, pseudo partner."

"Thank you. And ask her about the necklace," I said in a hushed voice as he walked toward the boat.

"You're telling me how to do my job again, Miss Pinkerton," he called back over his shoulder.

I wasn't versed on which side was starboard and which was portside, but as luck would have it, Detective Briggs, Theresa and William had their conversation on the side next to the pier. I tucked myself around the corner and managed to hear most of what they were saying. Especially with Theresa's tendency to talk loudly, that was, when she wasn't chewing her wad of gum.

Unfortunately, as loud and clear spoken as Theresa was, Detective Briggs kept his voice low and measured. I couldn't make out his words, but I didn't need to. The conversation quickly hurdled into

Theresa sobbing and sputtering words about protecting her husband. I was dying to hear more.

I scooted behind a pylon, deciding it was thick enough to hide me if I turned at an angle. Right then, a seagull landed on top of the pylon. It stared down at me with shiny black eyes, almost giving me a 'shame on you' look for eavesdropping. Or at least that was how I read the expression, and I was fairly versed in bird communication.

"I'd heard that Beverly died of suspicious circumstances, and I worried that William and I would be caught up in the investigation." Theresa said between sniffles. "I told you not to give her that darn necklace, you sentimental old fool. He went to the antique store to buy back that necklace because he wanted Beverly to have it again. High school sweethearts," Theresa sobbed. "It's ridiculous to hold on to old memories."

Detective Briggs said something else, and Theresa came right back confidently with her answer. "I was getting a tooth pulled at the dentist's office that afternoon. William was there to give me a ride home. You can check with Dr. Fenton."

Briggs said a few more words and then climbed down from the boat. I walked the long way around past the wharf shops and caught up with him at the end of the pier.

"You were snooping," he said.

"I tried. You really should learn to project when you talk. I couldn't make out anything you said. Theresa, on the other hand, sounded as if she was using a megaphone."

"Then you heard she had an alibi for the afternoon of the murder."

"An uncorroborated alibi," I added.

"It'll be easy enough to confirm."

"So Theresa did go in to search for the necklace. She thought it would get them in trouble, connect them to Beverly's death."

We walked down the steps of the pier. "Yes, it seems that way."

"I knew that someone had been rummaging through the jewelry box."

We stopped at his car, and he turned to me. "You're good at this kind of work, that's for sure. But if the dentist appointment is confirmed, we can cross Theresa off our list of suspects."

I pulled in my bottom lip to avoid too bright of a smile.

"I said 'we' again, didn't I?" He pulled his keys from his pocket.

"You did. But I'm not going to get overly excited about it. Good day, Detective Briggs."

"Good day, Miss Pinkerton."

CHAPTER 31

With Theresa quite possibly off the bubble list, I had to scratch her off my crude diagram of possible suspects and motives. That left just two people, Virginia and Daryl Featherton. But just as it was hard to imagine sweet, little Virginia bludgeoning the head of her neighbor, it was equally hard to find any direct motive for a seemingly successful business owner in the next town to have resorted to murder. The one thing that connected my narrow field of suspects was the pumpkin contest.

As much as I disliked the idea of having a chat with the mayor, it seemed since he was the judge, he might have some insight on the contest. After Detective Briggs drove off, I turned and headed along Pickford Way to the mayor's office. I wasn't certain he would see me because I didn't have an appointment. Even though it was a small town and I doubted his position was too taxing, he probably wouldn't just invite me in for a quick chat. Especially because he seemed to have formed a negative opinion of me long before actually getting to know me. I only hoped seeing me wouldn't remind him to look up obscure laws that would keep me from bringing Kingston to the shop.

It was a relatively quiet afternoon. Aside from a few high school kids hanging out at the town square listening to music and kicking a soccer ball around, the southwest corner of the town was nearly deserted. I took a moment to admire the lighthouse and come up with my excuse to see the mayor. I decided to ask if I was allowed to mail out flyers about the grand opening. I knew it was perfectly legal, but I could pretend I didn't. It might make him like me just a little better if he thought I was going to him for permission. He seemed like the kind of man who liked to be in charge of things.

I walked up the front steps of the building. The mayor's office was just a tiny brick house with white trimmed windows and columns to hold up the wide overhang. Some sorry looking geraniums were wilting in dark blue pots on the porch.

I walked inside. The receptionist looked up from her desk. The nameplate said Ms. Simpson. I'd seen the receptionist several times in passing, at the market and the diner. She was a tall, gangly, sixty something woman who had long fingers and a long nose to go with the rest of her. Her shoulders were hunched slightly forward. She looked up at me over her gold rimmed glasses.

"If you have a suggestion for the suggestion box, it's right over there on that side table. There are squares of paper and pens provided. But please don't walk off with a pen. Our office budget is tight." She went right back to her computer. Her long fingers flew over the keys. I walked to the suggestion box table and pretended to busy myself with a suggestion as I glanced around the room. I could hear a deep voice behind the door with the mayor's brass nameplate nailed to it. He was in. Ms. Simpson's desk was neatly organized with a red inbox basket, a white outbox basket and a blue finished work basket. The three baskets sat across the front of her desk in a patriotic red, white and blue display. It was quite possibly the only thing of color or charm in the otherwise bleak reception area. One wall had four portraits of stuffy looking old men, including Mayor Price. They were obviously the long proud line of Port Danby mayors. It was easy to see the family resemblance in their glowers.

I wrote a suggestion for the reception area in the mayor's office to be given a facelift so that it was more welcoming and charming like the shops on Harbor Lane. I pushed it into the box and walked confidently back up to her desk.

"I don't think we've met." I put out my hand. "I'm Lacey Pinkerton, new shop owner."

Annoyed by the interruption, she pulled her top lip down, stretching her nose even longer as she removed her glasses. "How do you do," she shook my hand. "Hannah Simpson."

"Nice to meet you. I was wondering if I could get a quick word with Mayor Price?"

"Certainly, let me just open the appointment window up." She reached for the computer mouse.

"Actually, this is just one question. It won't take but a minute. It's rather urgent because it is in regards to the grand opening of my flower shop."

I stood tall in front of her desk to let her know that I was resolute. She did the funny top lip stretch again and scooted back from her desk. "He's in a phone conference right now, but let me see if he has time."

She walked to the mayor's door, knocked twice and entered after he invited her inside. She shut the door behind her, which meant she was probably not going to speak favorably about my pushiness. I used it as an opportunity for some light snooping. There were several file folders and printed memos in the finished work basket. Everything was dated. Today's date was on the top memo. It was a brief memo to the council members mentioning that the pumpkin contest would continue as scheduled. I could still hear a conversation between the mayor and Ms. Simpson, but I couldn't make out the words.

I quickly fingered through the papers in the basket and saw that they were piled in order by date, with the latest date on top. My fingertip grazed over a thick sheet of vellum. I pushed aside the papers on top of it. It was a nicely printed certificate of award for the first place winner of the pumpkin contest. Strangely enough, the name Virginia Hopkins was already printed on the line in a fancy script style font. I pushed back the paper directly on top of it. It was dated three days before the murder. Apparently, the mayor was clairvoyant enough to know who would win the contest weeks before the actual event.

The door opened. I stepped back from the basket and desk and grasped my hands behind my back. I smiled.

There was no return smile. Ms. Simpson walked to her desk and sat down. "As I've said before, I can make an appointment for you. The mayor has no spare time on his agenda today."

"Actually, never mind. I think I've answered the question myself. Nice meeting you." I could feel her confused gaze on my back as I hurried out of the office.

CHAPTER 32

*N*evermore had positioned himself on the kitchen rug so that I had to walk around him as I baked chocolate chip cookies. After my brief failed visit to the mayor's office, I'd stopped at the police station. Officer Chinmoor, who looked grumpy from behind a mountain of paperwork, said Detective Briggs had been called away to Mayfield, a town just east of Port Danby. I was disappointed that I wouldn't have a chance to tell him about the preprinted pumpkin certificate. So I headed home and decided to continue my quest for information. Dashwood had mentioned that Helen Voight was also a judge in the contest. (*Although one could hardly consider it a contest if the winner was pre-chosen.*) Helen lived at the end of Loveland Terrace in a cute yellow house. I'd seen her drive past my house a few times in her bright blue car. We had waved politely to each other, but there had not been a formal introduction. The chocolate chip cookies were a nice neighborly gesture and a perfect excuse to have a chat. I only knew a few details about Helen and her husband, Gary. Their three kids had already left home for college and careers, and they both worked at a bank in Chesterton.

My cat's ears perked up as I filled a plate with cookies, taking time to eat one or two myself along the way. I was still getting used to the oven in my new place, but the cookies had turned out nicely. Nevermore popped up to his paws and curled himself around my legs.

"Never, when have I ever fed you chocolate chip cookies?" I reached into the cupboard for one of his chicken flavored treats. Kingston made a cooing sound the second he heard the foil package rattle. I fed them each a treat and covered Kingston's cage for the night.

I checked my hair in the entryway mirror. It was a waste of time because of the mass of curls would be made even wilder by the evening fog. Maybe Lola had a good point about the hats.

I walked out into the cool night air with my plate of warm cookies and headed down the street. Helen's house was at the end where the street curved into a cul-de-sac. The short walk gave me some time to gently formulate a few questions about the pumpkin contest.

A flickering television light glowed through the front window. I walked up the pathway and up the steps. A cute painted sign made of wooden letters and spelling out *welcome* hung over the dark blue front door. The shutters along the front windows were also painted dark blue, a nice contrast to the yellow facade.

I knocked on the door and wondered if I'd get Mr. Voight instead of Helen. I heard the latch of a peephole open. I put on my best smile. The door swung open. Helen's smile grew wider when she noticed I was holding a plate covered in foil.

"I'm Lacey Pinkerton. I just thought it was time to come by and introduce myself," I said. "I don't want to intrude on your night, but here are some cookies."

Helen had one of those soft pillowy faces that made it hard to see any cheekbones or chin line. Her blue eyes were sparkly and kind, and she had long brown hair that was tied back with a hair scrunchy.

"Aren't you sweet. I'm the one that should have introduced myself to you." She took the plate of cookies. "Just like I think I was supposed to be the person delivering the cookies. I'd introduce to you to Gary, but he's busy watching football right now." She followed with an eye roll. "Can't get his attention for five seconds with that game on."

"I can't stay anyhow. I just wanted to let you know that I'm just on the end if you need anything. And don't worry if there's a shifty eyed crow hanging around the street. It's just my pet, Kingston."

She laughed loud enough to earn a shush from her husband in the next room.

Helen turned her face that direction. "Shush yourself, Gary, or I won't fix you any cheese dip for the game." She turned back to me. "I've heard all about the crow. I think it's wonderful. You hardly need to bother with Halloween decorations when you have a live raven to perch on your porch."

"I hadn't thought of that."

Her pillowy face smoothed some and her brow flattened. "You poor thing, I heard you were the person to discover Beverly out in her pumpkin patch." There was a hitch in her voice during the last few words. She fanned her face with her free hand. "You'll have to forgive me. It's still so hard to believe she's gone."

"It's very sad." It turned out I didn't need to come up with a way to bring up the contest. Helen had given me an opening. "Have you heard whether or not the pumpkin contest has been cancelled? I've heard you were a judge."

Her generous smile faded, and her lips pulled tight and thin. "I'm not sure, and I'm no longer a judge." She turned her head into the house. "I'll be right there, Gary," she called to her husband. Even though I'd heard his shush, I hadn't heard him call her.

Helen backed up. "I need to fix him his snacks. Thank you so much for the cookies. It's been a delight meeting you." She spoke so quickly I didn't have a chance to respond.

Seconds later I was standing in front of the shut blue door.

"Well, that was interesting," I mumbled to myself as I turned around and headed home.

CHAPTER 33

$\mathcal{I}$'d thought it and *boom*, it happened. Only it was Elsie and not Les who decided to invest in some colorful seat cushions to go on the outdoor chairs. She had just finished tying on the last one when I stepped out to walk to the corner market.

She waved her hand around the patio area. "Ta da! What do you think?"

"I still say it's your scones, cupcakes and cookies that bring people to your shop, Elsie. But I'm sure customers will be more than pleased to rest their bottoms on something soft while they nibble on a ginger scone."

"I think so too. And Les just has those cold hard seats, so I'm sure his coffee drinkers will wander over here to sit."

I smiled. "I'm sure you're right. I'm on my way to the market. Gigi put out a new batch of pumpkins. I've decided to buy one for the store window."

"That's a good idea. I'm just about to start baking my pumpkin shaped sugar cookies. Drop by later for a sample."

"I certainly will." The sun had come up early today. It was unseasonably warm as I headed along the sidewalk to the market. I was disappointed to see Detective Briggs' car was not parked in front of the police station. He had been busy with some other cases and had been neglecting the Port Danby murder. It seemed I needed to pick up the slack some. I had plenty to tell him but nothing definitive. Nothing that stood out like a smoking gun. Nothing that said, 'ah ha, this is exactly what happened'.

I wondered if Beverly's murder would ever be solved or if it would eventually fade into one of those cold cases. That thought depressed me. No victim should end up a big question mark in a storage box at the back of the police station.

With that, I was more determined than ever to find out what'd happened to Beverly Kent. Maybe it would help to take another look and sniff around Beverly's farm.

My pumpkin decision didn't take long. I grabbed one nice jolly ten pounder and hauled it inside to pay. Tom Upton was busy sweeping up a bag of cheese puffs that had broken on the floor. He had to work hard to sweep them up before the dachshunds, Molly and Buddy, gobbled them.

I couldn't stop a laugh. "Maybe you should just throw in the towel and let them clean up for you."

Tom pushed the dogs back and kept sweeping. "I would if I didn't know that in three hours I'd be cleaning up orange tinted dog barf. Gigi," he called. "Come ring up Lacey's pumpkin."

Gigi hurried out. "Just one? What about for your house?"

"Uh, I hadn't thought of that."

"Gigi, stop pestering people about the pumpkins," Tom said over the cloud of cheese dust. "We can always sell them after Halloween for pumpkin pie. We both ended up ordering pumpkins. Now we have way too many."

"Tell you what, I will buy two for my porch later this week."

"You're the kind of customer we love." Gigi smiled as she handed me back my change.

I carried my newest orange buddy out of the store and back to the shop. I set the pumpkin down below the potter's table until I could figure out exactly how to decorate it. Kingston dropped down from his perch and sauntered over to the strange new addition. He circled it and pecked at it a few times, but soon grew bored and returned to his window.

I'd gotten an idea to dress up my marigold pots with some thin orange and black ribbon, and I had a few more to finish. I reached forward to the spools of ribbon. As I brought my arm back, my elbow pushed the potted plant off the table. It landed directly on the pumpkin before hitting the floor and shattering into shards of broken pottery, mounds of dirt and broken marigolds.

"Darn it." I stooped down to start picking up the shards and noticed that the filled pot had barely even registered as a mark on the thick pumpkin shell. As I finished cleaning up, I thought about how badly destroyed Beverly's prize pumpkin had been. It had already been determined that Beverly died from a blow to her head. The injury had nothing to do with the pumpkin. Yet the pumpkin was smashed open.

I grabbed the broom to clean up the rest of the mess. Clean up the mess. Someone killed Beverly and then tried to 'clean it up' by making it look like an accident. Or maybe Beverly caught them smashing the pumpkin, and she tried to stop them. And a tussle followed. There were more answers out in that pumpkin patch. My nose and I were going to take a ride out to look for them.

CHAPTER 34

I'd locked up and was about to climb on my bike to head out to Beverly's farm when I spotted Briggs' car out front of the station. He had certainly been scarce lately, and there were things I needed to tell him. I rested my bike against my bench and walked in the direction of the station.

Franki's Diner was busy for breakfast. As I swept along the crowded parking lot, I glimpsed a small white pick-up with a magnetic sign on the door. It was from Featherton's nursery. I took a detour and turned up the path to the diner entrance. I didn't need to snoop too long into the front windows. Daryl Featherton was seated at the first table by the window with a plate of steak and eggs in front of him. Both the eggs and the meat were swimming in Franki's special ketchup.

I glanced across the street. Briggs' car was still out front, but there was no sign of him. I didn't want to miss talking to him. It seemed I had time to buy an iced tea and do a little snooping along with it.

I walked inside and was blasted with the usual smell of bacon, eggs and maple syrup, a pleasing combination for the average nose, but for me it was somewhat overwhelming. I worked to shut down my senses and walked to the counter.

Franki and her servers were busy. I hated to bother them for an iced tea that I really didn't need, but I had a plan. I peeked over my shoulder at Featherton. Fortunately, he was too involved in his breakfast to notice me. The unwieldy gauze and tape on his arm had been replaced by two bandages. The cut was on the top side of his forearm, an odd place for an injury. Aside from a half empty bottle of ketchup on the table, there was a cup of coffee, a glass of orange juice and, most importantly, a stack of napkins. And from the looks of his fingers, he hadn't bothered to use one.

"What can I get you, Lacey?" Franki asked.

I turned back toward her. "Just an iced tea to go please. If it's not too much bother."

She wiped her forehead with the back of her forearm. "Nope, we're all caught up now." She left and returned with an iced tea. I grabbed a sugar packet from the container and plucked the lid off the cup to add the sweetener. I went to snap the cap back on the cup and tipped it just enough to splash tea on the floor.

Daryl glanced at the spilled tea, then got right back to his breakfast.

"Excuse me." I reached for one of the napkins on his table. "Do you mind if I borrow a napkin?"

"Take 'em all. I don't need them." He glanced up just for a second and seemed to finally recognize me. "You're the flower shop owner."

"Yes, nice to see you." I crouched down, cleaned the floor and walked out with my tea.

Now there was one more thing on my list for Detective Briggs. Daryl Featherton eats at the diner, and he loves Franki's ketchup.

The napkin aversion didn't gel in my head until I stepped up on the curb in front of the station. Detective Briggs was just walking out.

He pulled his sunglasses down over his brown eyes. His eyes were nice, but the man did looking dapper in sunglasses. The sunglasses quickly reminded me of a college professor who I'd had a little crush on. He always came to class in sunglasses.

"Professor Dunbar." His name popped from my mouth before I could stop it.

Briggs turned around as if he thought maybe Professor Dunbar was behind him. He turned back to face me. "And good morning to you too, Miss Pinkerton."

"Professor Dunbar, of course. Why didn't I think of it before?"

"I don't know?" Briggs said as a question, rightly confused with my one-sided conversation.

"Professor Dunbar was my microbiology professor. He had the best handlebar moustache and dreamy blue eyes that could look right into your soul. But I digress."

He pinched his forefinger and thumb together. "Just a little bit."

"Microbiology lab requires a lot of hand washing in a harsh sanitizer so that samples aren't contaminated. Professor Dunbar's hands were always rough and raw. The university had to supply him with baby soft hand towels because the paper towels in the lab were too harsh and painful on his chapped hands."

"Miss Pinkerton, I was just on my way out, so if that's all you needed to say—"

"No," I said abruptly. "I'm getting to my point. And it's a doozy. I was just in the diner where Daryl Featherton was eagerly eating a breakfast of steak and eggs . . . doused in Franki's ketchup. And he wasn't using his napkins, even though, trust me, he needed to.

"When I spoke to him at the nursery, he was busy washing his hands. Then he shook them dry. I offered to get him a paper towel but he said no. Featherton's hands are too rough and chapped from gardening for paper towels. Just like dreamy eyed Professor Dunbar." I finally stopped to draw in a breath.

Briggs' gaze flicked across the street to the diner. Featherton's truck was still in the parking lot. "So someone who likes to eat Franki's ketchup and who hates to use napkins might have touched Beverly's blouse, explaining how she got the ketchup stain. It's flimsy but plausible."

I tapped my arm. "He took off the gauze and replaced it with two bandages. Maybe a wound from an angry woman yielding a hoe? I think Beverly caught Daryl smashing her prize pumpkin and a fight ensued. That was my original reason for coming over here until I saw

Featherton's truck at the diner and wondered if he was eating ketchup."

Detective Briggs smiled and shook his head. "When I saw you, I was going to ask what was new since I'd been out of town."

"Where have you been anyhow? We've got a murder case to solve."

"I haven't forgotten about poor Beverly Kent. It's just other crimes do take place outside of Port Danby. I was in Mayfield testifying in a case I worked on last month. Is there anything else?"

I laughed. "How long do you have?"

"I'm just on my way out to Beverly's farm to have a look around. Would you like to join me? Then you can fill me in on everything else."

"Why, I thought you'd never ask."

Detective Briggs opened the passenger door and I climbed inside. He leaned down. "And before you ask—we're not putting on the siren." He shut the door.

There was a nice blue and green necktie draped over the console. It had one of those permanent knots that had been pushed down for easy removal.

Detective Briggs sat behind the wheel. I lifted the tie. "I see you're one of those men who prefers to leave his tie knotted and ready to wear. I'll bet you look very nice in a tie."

He took the tie from my hand and tossed it onto the backseat. "They require it in the courthouse. And yes, I leave it knotted. Saves me about an hour of frustration trying to get the thing tied right. I swear my dad used to do it one handed while he brushed his teeth, but I can't do it even with a diagram pasted to the bathroom mirror."

I looked over at him. "It takes a brave, confident man to admit that."

His laugh was low and deep like his voice. Briggs pulled out onto Harbor Lane and turned the corner along Pickford Way. "Theresa's alibi checked out, by the way. She was at the dentist."

"I've forgotten all about Theresa. I still think the whole murder is tied to the pumpkin contest. It's seems farfetched that a woman could be killed for growing an enormous orange squash, but while you were busy in Mayfield, I was busy here in Port Danby. I went to see my least favorite person, Mayor Price. Of course he wouldn't see me because I didn't have an appointment."

"Why would you go to see Mayor Price?"

"Dash mentioned that Mayor Price and Helen Voight, a neighbor on Loveland Terrace, are the judges for the pumpkin contest."

"Dash told you, eh?"

"Yes." I looked over at him. Just hearing the name Dash seemed to make his mood sour. "Anyhow, I didn't get to see the mayor, but while his assistant was in his office, I took the liberty to snoop around."

Briggs shook his head. "You've got to stop doing that, Lacey. You're going to get into trouble."

I ignored the warning because I was too shocked to hear him say my name.

He took my stunned silence as anger. "Someone will catch you rifling through their stuff and—"

"You called me Lacey."

He paused. "Did I? Sorry."

"No, I like the way you say it. Hey, since we're kind of partnering up, maybe you could call me that all the time and I could call you James."

"Nope. Keep going. You were snooping and . . ."

"The mayor's assistant, Ms. Simpson, is as neat and organized as she is unfriendly. I fingered through the papers in her finished work basket. The papers were all in order, earlier dates at the bottom. On top was yesterday's memo letting the city council members know that despite the tragedy, the contest was not cancelled. Farther down in the stack, below the date of Beverly's untimely death, was a nicely printed sheet of vellum. It was the first place certificate for the pumpkin contest. And Virginia's name was already printed on it."

Briggs' face snapped my direction. "Really? You're sure it was for the pumpkin contest?"

"Unless there are some other contests I don't know about, it was for the Port Danby Pumpkin Contest. Weird, right?"

"I'd say so. Obviously, someone had fixed the contest. I guess I better talk to the mayor."

"Yes indeed. But don't tell him I was snooping. He already doesn't trust me and my million dollar nose."

Briggs parked in front of Beverly's farm. "Mayor Price is not the most open minded individual in the world, but for what it's worth, I trust you and your million dollar nose implicitly."

"Thank you."

"That's why I need to question Franki and find out if Featherton was in the diner the morning of Beverly's murder. Now let's see if we missed anything out in that pumpkin patch."

CHAPTER 35

*D*etective Briggs and I pushed dirt and leaves around, not certain what we were looking for. A big, sprawling pumpkin patch was not an easy place to find evidence. Beverly's gigantic pumpkin had become food for insects and any bird willing to cross paths with the Regency dressed scarecrow. The outer shell had become soft and mushy. I pressed on it, and it collapsed even more.

"I forgot about my pumpkin incident at the shop," I said as I sifted around in the dirt, sniffing for anything that wasn't a pumpkin plant or soil smell.

Briggs was walking around the perimeter of the fencing. "You had a pumpkin incident?"

"A potted plant fell off the counter and landed on the pumpkin I bought from the market. The pot shattered, but the pumpkin was left virtually untouched. It just made me realize how tough pumpkins were."

Briggs stooped down and pushed aside a particularly thick tangle of vines and leaves. "They are tough. I don't know about you, but as a kid I could have lost an eye a thousand times all in the pursuit of making the scariest jack-o'-lantern. Even broke one of my mom's sharpest knives once."

"See, proof that Beverly's pumpkin had been destroyed long before her head ended up inside of it."

"Yes, I think that was already established."

I walked over to the gate where I'd found the hoe. Maybe I'd missed something there. "Do you think someone killed her and then moved her over to the smashed pumpkin to make it look like she fell into it?"

"Seems that way."

"Briggs, have they found out whose blood is on the hoe?"

He shook his head. "No matches in the criminal database, but that still leaves millions of possibilities."

"But we know someone in Port Danby who was recently injured."

Briggs looked up from his search through the vines. "Featherton."

"Yes."

"Sure wish I knew what was used to kill Beverly. The coroner said it was the edge of something very solid. But whatever it was, it doesn't seem to be in the garden."

I reached down and picked up a clump of dirt near the gate that had a few pumpkin seeds stuck in it. "Strange, I wonder how these seeds got here. Maybe someone dragged them here on the bottom of their shoe." I straightened and as I did, I got a whiff of a metallic smell.

"Blood," I said excitedly. "I smell blood."

Briggs hurried over. "Where is it?"

I held up my hand. "Just a second." I stooped back down and then slowly straightened. "Here at the top edge of the fence post. That's where it's most concentrated."

Briggs lifted his sunglasses to get a closer look. "The splintery, coarse surface of the weathered post makes it hard to see any stain. I'll get my swab kit from the car. Good work. That nose is small, but it sure comes in handy."

I glanced from the post to the broken pumpkin. "I wonder if this was where she hit her head. Beverly caught someone destroying the pumpkin. She went after them with her garden hoe and got in one good swing before the person shoved her. She fell against the post and then the pumpkin destroyer realized she was dead. They decided to cover their pumpkin destroying tracks at the same time and made it look as if she'd fallen into her pumpkin."

"That's a good scenario, Miss Pinkerton. Now we need evidence to connect the killer to the scene." He walked back to his car.

I pushed my hair behind my ears as it kicked around in the breeze. As I turned to face the wind to keep the hair out of my face, I spotted Virginia Hopkins walking quickly across the yard. As she drew nearer, I could see that she was crying.

She tromped through the lantana and seemed to know exactly where to walk for the best footing. Her sobs rolled across the yard. I glanced back and was relieved to see Briggs returning with his evidence kit. He heard the loud sobs too and picked up his pace to catch up to where I was standing.

"Do you think we're about to hear a confession of some sort? She wasn't nearly this upset on the day we found Beverly."

"Seems like it." Briggs lowered his voice because Virginia was nearly at the gate.

"I did it," she blurted between sobs and deep, shuddering breaths. "I did it."

Detective Briggs stepped through the gate. "I need you to calm yourself and tell me exactly what you did."

"I've been living with such terrible guilt. I can't eat or sleep or even look out the window toward this farm." She covered her face and her shoulders shuddered.

"Virginia, should I get you a glass of water?" I suggested.

She shook her head. "No, I don't deserve water." She thrust her hands out in front of her. "Cuff me and take me in. I'm guilty."

"Mrs. Hopkins, I need you to tell me exactly what you did," Detective Briggs said in a cool, smooth voice.

Virginia took another deep breath and let it out. "I cut the pumpkin from the vine. There. It's out. I cut Beverly's prize pumpkin from its vine." She shook her hands in front of him. "Cuff me."

Briggs shot me an amused look. "Mrs. Hopkins, that's hardly a bad enough crime to warrant handcuffs or arrest."

"But I did it hoping my pumpkin could pass it up. My pumpkin needed to win. He was counting on it. He was so mad when he heard that Beverly's pumpkin was bigger."

"He? Who are you talking about?" Briggs asked.

"Why, that awful Mr. Featherton. If my pumpkin didn't win the contest, then his contract with the seed company would fall through. And now poor Beverly is dead." She covered her face to sob again.

I walked over and put my arm around her shoulders. "Let's get you inside for a glass of water. Detective Briggs has some work to do. Then I'm sure he'll come in and talk to you some more."

CHAPTER 36

I fidgeted with the hem of my shirt as we drove back to
Harbor Lane. I sensed that Detective Briggs was holding in
a laugh or some comment that contained the word *rookie*. And that's
exactly what I was. I'd never been part of a murder investigation. As
the pieces started falling into place and we drew nearer to a suspect,
nervous excitement swept over me. We were heading back to town
and very likely closing in on a killer. It was ridiculous to be giddy, but
I couldn't help myself. And my mom was certain I'd get bored in Port
Danby. That thought, along with the dizzy rush in my head, pushed
out an involuntary and ill-timed laugh.

Briggs looked over at me. "Something funny?"

"No, sorry. Just thinking about my mom warning me I'd be bored
in a small town."

"Ah yes. Guess she didn't see you as a super sleuth."

"I suppose not. I'll bet after Beverly saw the vine cut on her
pumpkin she went to the farm supply store to rent the thingamabob
to move her pumpkin some place safe."

"The skid steer? Yes that's what I think too. And she probably
thought Featherton had cut the vine or put Virginia up to it. That's
why they argued at the nursery."

"Exactly. Where to first?" I looked over at him with my best wide-eyed expectant face, hoping it would keep him from telling me I was done with the investigation at this point.

It seemed to work. He sighed in surrender. "First, I want to ask Franki if Featherton was in the diner the day of the murder. It'll help connect him to the ketchup stain on her blouse. Then I'm heading to the mayor's office to see what was up with the contest. After Virginia's slightly hysterical confession, Featherton's motive seems clear. He needed his hybrid pumpkin to win the contest to seal the deal with the seed distributor. Money and success are usually clear cut motives. I'm wondering if Featherton saw that Beverly's pumpkin was going to win, and he decided to take the easier, less messy route first and bribe the judge."

"Judges," I added.

"Judges?"

"Yes, Helen Voight, remember? And I've already talked to her. Of course she had no idea of my intent when I strolled up to her house with a neighborly plate of cookies."

"You made cookies?"

"I bake. I'm not just a walking million dollar nose. I have many talents."

"I've noticed. Go on."

"Helen was quite friendly and sweet but when I brought up the pumpkin contest, she made some excuse to end the chat. She said she wasn't going to be a judge and then just about slammed her front door in my face."

"Interesting."

Briggs parked in front of the police station, and we walked across the street to the diner. Franki was filling coffee pots. She smiled when she saw Briggs and was more than a little surprised to see me standing next to him.

She walked over. "The usual, Detective Briggs?"

"No thanks, Franki. I'm here on business. Can you tell me whether or not Daryl Featherton was in the diner on Monday, the day of Beverly's murder?"

"Oh, that's easy. Daryl comes in here every Monday because he makes a delivery to a big garden store in Mayfield. He stops in for his usual steak and eggs whenever he's heading through town." She cast an inquisitive look my direction. I just smiled in return.

"Thank you, Franki." I followed Briggs out.

"That's a big deal, right?" I asked as I hurried to keep up with his fast strides.

"Could be." We got back into his car.

"We could just walk," I noted.

"Official business, remember?"

"You're right. Wouldn't be right to just stroll up to the mayor's office during official business."

We drove along Pickford Way and pulled up to the mayor's office. I reached for the door handle. "Miss Pinkerton, I'm going inside alone."

I sat back in disappointment. "Probably a good idea."

"Glad you agree," he said with just a twinge of sarcasm. He stepped out of the car and climbed the steps.

"If only I were a fly on the wall," I mumbled to myself. I sat up sharply. "Or a citizen with a suggestion for the suggestion box." I glanced around to make sure no one saw me step out of the detective's car. The mayor's office was far enough in the corner of town that there were rarely any cars or people around. I knew Briggs would scowl when he saw me, but I just couldn't stop myself.

I opened the office door. I assumed Detective Briggs would be meeting the mayor inside his office, but the two men were standing in the reception area. Ms. Simpson wasn't at her desk. It was possible she'd stepped out. The expected scowl came my way from Briggs, but I ignored it and both men as I walked confidently over to the suggestion box.

I picked up a piece of paper and stared at it, unsure of my suggestion.

"Could we talk in your office, Mayor Price?" Briggs shot me an annoyed sideways glance as the two men disappeared behind the closed door. I moved closer to the door to listen in, but it was just two deep voices mumbling behind a solid door. Seconds later, the mayor's voice grew louder. He was angry.

"I don't appreciate this line of questioning, James," he snapped. "Yes, Featherton came to me hoping to arrange the contest, but I told him no. Helen was made so nervous by it all, she decided not to judge this year. Now, if you'll excuse me." The office door opened. "I have a lot to do." Mayor Price followed Briggs out. His face grew red when he saw me still standing in the reception area.

I waved the suggestion paper in my hand. "Still thinking." Then I did something stupid. I was, after all, a rookie. "Why is there a first place certificate printed for Virginia when the contest hasn't even taken place?" The question shot out.

The red in the mayor's face turned nearly purple. "Were you snooping around Ms. Simpson's desk?"

Detective Briggs was shooting me a look that let me know he was almost as angry as the mayor. I deserved it.

"I—excuse me, but I saw a piece of vellum paper in the basket. It was exactly what I wanted for the flyers for my shop. I fingered through the stack just to touch it and feel the quality." I was getting just a bit too good at lying, and it bothered me . . . a little. Besides, it was all in the name of solving a murder.

The color had still not washed from the mayor's face as he marched over to the basket and reached inside. He pulled out the certificate with Virginia's name. Then he slid it aside to reveal a second certificate with Beverly's name. "It is always one of them, so we print the certificates up ahead of time to have them ready to hand out that day."

"Yes, that makes sense." My face was warm from an embarrassed blush. I placed the blank suggestion paper on the table and made my way to the door. If I'd had a tail, it would have been hanging down between my legs.

"Thank you for your time, Mayor Price," Detective Briggs said. "I won't—"

The front door opened just as I reached for it. Daryl Featherton walked in. He looked at Mayor Price and then his stunned face turned to Detective Briggs.

"Mr. Featherton," Briggs spoke up. "I need to ask you a few—"

Featherton didn't wait for him to finish. He spun around and shoved me out of the way. I fell back on my bottom as Detective Briggs raced after him. I pushed to my feet and smiled weakly at the mayor before running out of the office.

Detective Briggs had Featherton with his arm behind his back. He walked him to the car, reading him his rights.

"I didn't go there to kill her," Featherton blurted. "I just wanted to destroy that damn pumpkin so I wouldn't lose the contract. Beverly attacked me first with the hoe. I pushed her and she fell against the post and hit her head. I didn't plan to kill her."

Detective Briggs handcuffed Featherton and led him to the back-seat of the car. He slammed the door shut and finally looked my direction. I braced for his angry lecture.

"I'll just walk home from here," I said quietly.

He looked at me for a long moment. "Good work, Miss Pinkerton." He walked around, climbed into his car and drove off with the suspect slouched angrily in the backseat.

CHAPTER 37

*H*ot cocoa and a seat on the porch seemed like the perfect way to end a long day. I certainly hadn't expected my first big occasion in the shop to be a funeral, but I was glad to be able to provide flowers for Beverly's small service at Graystone Church. All of her neighbors came to say good-bye and support her sister, Beverly's only living relative.

Nevermore rubbed back and forth along my legs as I gazed out at the dark sky. It was a fogless night and a blanket of stars twinkled like diamonds in a navy blue carpet. The cat's head popped up at a sound. He trotted off to investigate.

Dash's front door opened and closed. He walked out with Captain. They headed over to my front yard. Dash stopped in front of the steps. He was wearing one of his usual flannel shirts and a hint of a smile.

I held up my cup of cocoa. "I could make you one."

"No thanks. Rumors have been swirling that you helped solve Beverly's murder."

"With a little help from my nose. I confess, it was very intriguing work. I'm beginning to think I missed my calling."

He laughed. "Well, I'm sure you'll find other intriguing ways to keep yourself busy. You seem like the kind of person who doesn't like to just sit and relax."

I lifted the cocoa again to show him he was wrong. "I like relaxing just fine, but I also like a bit of intrigue. In fact, I think now that this case is solved, I might delve into the Hawksworth Manor murder. Just for fun."

He laughed again. "I get the feeling life around Port Danby is not going to be the same now that Lacey 'Pink' Pinkerton has moved to town."

Lacey 'Pink' Pinkerton, the local flower shop owner, is thrilled to supply colorful flower arrangements for the Third Annual Food Fair being held in the Port Danby town square. But when one of the well-known but not so well-loved bloggers is found dead in her motel room, Lacey steps in to help Detective James Briggs solve the case. (Whether he likes it or not.)

Carnations and Chaos (Port Danby Cozy Mystery #2) coming October 17th, 2017.

ELSIE'S SUGAR AND SPICE PUMPKIN BREAD

View the recipe online:
https://www.londonlovett.com/recipe-box/

Elsie's Sugar and Spice
PUMPKIN BREAD

Ingredients:

Bread:
1 1/2 cup + 2 Tbsp all-purpose flour
1 tsp baking soda
1/2 tsp salt
1 tsp spice mixture (see spice mixture)
1 1/2 cup granulated sugar
1 cup canned pumpkin
1/2 cup vegetable oil
2 eggs
1/3 cup water

Cream Cheese Ribbon:
4 oz cream cheese, softened
2 Tbsp granulated sugar
1 Tbsp all-purpose flour
1 egg yolk
2 tsp milk

Spice mixture (May be substituted with 2 tsp pumpkin pie spice):
1 tsp cinnamon
1/4 tsp all spice
1/2 tsp ground ginger
1/4 tsp nutmeg

Sugar and Spice Nut Topping:
3/4 cup chopped pecans
1 tsp spice mixture (see spice mixture)
1/3 cup granulated sugar
2 Tbsp brown sugar

Directions:

1. Preheat over to 350°

2. Prepare spice mixture: combine all spice mixture ingredients in a small bowl, set aside

3. **Sugar and Spice Nut Topping:** Chop 3/4 cup pecans. Mix together 1 tsp of the spice mixture, 1/3 cup sugar and 2 Tbsp brown sugar in a small bowl. Add chopped pecans to the bowl and stir to combine. Set aside.

4. **Combine dry bread ingredients:** In a large bowl, mix together 1 1/2 cup+ 2 Tbsp all-purpose flour, 1 tsp baking soda, 1/2 tsp salt, 1 tsp spice mixture and 1 1/2 cup granulated sugar. Once the ingredients are well mixed, make a well in the center of the dry ingredient bowl. Set aside.

5. **Combine wet bread ingredients:** In a medium bowl, whisk together 1 cup canned pumpkin, 1/2 cup vegetable oil, 2 eggs and 1/3 cup water.

6. **Prepare bread batter:** Pour the wet ingredient mixture into the well in the dry ingredient bowl. Use a wooden spoon to mix until just combined. (Make sure not to over mix here or you'll end up with chewy pumpkin bread.)

7. **Cream cheese mixture:** In a medium bowl, add 4 ounces softened cream cheese, 2 Tbsp granulated sugar, 1 Tbsp flour, 1 egg yolk and 2 tsp milk. Use an electric mixer to whip the ingredients together until smooth and creamy.

8. **Assemble the bread:** Prepare a 9 x 5 inch loaf pan with non-stick spray. Pour half of the pumpkin bread batter into the pan. Use a rubber spatula or spoon to scoop the cream cheese mixture on top of the batter. Spread it out as evenly as possible. Sprinkle 1/2 of the sugar and spice nut mixture on top of the cream cheese layer. Scoop the rest of the pumpkin bread batter on top of the nut layer and spread out evenly. Sprinkle the remaining 1/2 of the sugar and spice nut mixture evenly on top.

9. **Baking: 60-70 minutes:** Tent the loaf pan with foil for the first 25 minutes of baking (this will prevent the sugary topping from burning). After 25 minutes, remove the foil and bake for another 35 minutes. Start checking the loaf after 1 hour of baking time. Poke the loaf with a toothpick or fork to test if it's ready. Once the bread is done the toothpick or fork will come out clean. (I began checking at 1 hour, and my loaf was baked to perfection at 1 hour and 10 minutes--time my vary slightly depending on your oven and bakeware.)

10. **Cool down:** Let the pumpkin bread sit and cool down in the loaf pan before removing it.
Slice, serve and enjoy!

ABOUT THE AUTHOR

London Lovett is the author of the new Port Danby Cozy Mystery series. She loves getting caught up in a good mystery and baking delicious new treats!

Facebook.com/LondonLovettWrites
www.londonlovett.com
londonlovettwrites@gmail.com

90999123R00110

Made in the USA
San Bernardino, CA
24 October 2018